A Love Story
with
a Little
Heartbreak

A Love Story
with
a Little Heartbreak

Thomas Dunker

Stormy River Publishing

Stormy River Publishing

Cover Art: © Linnea Pergola, www.LinneaPergola-art.com

ISBN: 978-0-578-02914-6

ACKNOWLEDGEMENTS

Grateful acknowledgement to Stewart Bick, M.D. for his medical counsel and enlightening insights; to Jerry Kurth and Gina Lake, who provided some details of this story; and to Linnea Barnes, who provided encouragement and support throughout the writing of this story along with some great insights and beautiful cover art.

To my mother

CHAPTER ONE

It was at that very moment, the moment that Connie altered the placement of a few strands of her blonde hair, when her eyes locked into the eyes of the image staring back at her in the mirror, her image. The image had an intensity she wasn't feeling, and suddenly it spoke to her, although her own face remained perfectly still. It said, "You will never see me again."

CHAPTER TWO

In late 1945, euphoria over our nation's victory in the war hung in the air still, even though the country was focused on working hard to move forward with a steady rhythm of normalcy and promise and a single-minded commitment to return to the goings on of life as it should be—as the soldiers on the battlefields had dreamed it would be if they were victorious. That euphoria lingered was entirely understandable, knowing that only a couple of years earlier the future of America had been in doubt—for that matter, the very existence of America. Yes! The threat of Nazi dominion loomed for several years in the mid-forties, and prospects became even scarier when the diabolical union between the Nazis and Imperial Japan resulted in the attack on Pearl Harbor.

By 1946, a pronounced vitality had returned, a spring in people's steps could be seen once again and an effervescent joy over the return to sanity. People were making new lives, making out, and making babies. You have to know that all this "making" activity had been on hold during the years the nation was at war. Now it was in full swing, and love permeated the air along with that euphoria.

But what do I know? Not much really. I wasn't around in the forties. I wasn't born until 1951, which now seems like as long ago as World War Two, or even World War One. Going much farther back than thirty years puts everything on the same plane in my memory as simply "a long time ago," just like I would say the Civil War was a long time ago. Of course, I didn't have to experience the Civil War to know about it; that's what history books are for. Even better than history books, at least for the kind of history I'm writing about here, is word of mouth.

This story is, in part, hearsay. Like I said, I didn't exist in the forties, but I learned a lot about people who did live in that period because I talked to them years later, some of them anyway. Mostly, I learned about that time from my mother because this story is her story, which I have now told often enough that I feel I was there with her in 1946 and the years that followed, even though I didn't really make it onto the scene until 1951, as I said—if coming out of the birth canal can be called making it onto the scene. Of course, many of the blanks were filled in by others who were firsthand witnesses to the events, so that might explain why it may seem that I know a lot more than what you might think. And the rest—well, that's what imaginations are for, right? I'm pretty good at filling in the blanks.

I have a really good imagination, something I've always been thankful for. And I can tell a really good story, something a lot of my friends have been thankful for. This story has had an effect on everyone I have ever told it to, so I can't imagine why it wouldn't affect you too.

Personally, I've known about much of this story since I was a teenager in the sixties because I made it a point to be my family's historian, something of a family snoop, since I was self-appointed and assumed the role, essentially without anyone's awareness or knowledge of that appointment.

You see, writing a book is an interesting endeavor into the unknown. Outlines help, of course, but in my humble experience, what often makes it onto the printed page is something never foreseen by the writer. Without getting too ahead of myself, as I have mentioned, the adventure you're about to read is my mother's story. Her name was Connie Ortlieb. Her story is one that has been my own personal source of courage over the years. I got my courage from my mother, most of it anyway. She's the one who taught me to pick myself up from a fall and get on with life. I've fallen many times, but none matched what she went through. Courage is a wonderful, wonderful thing, and it may actually exist in all of us, although I'm not absolutely sure about that. Some know it is in them and some don't until the moment they have to call on it. But I digress.

CHAPTER THREE

It was the tail end of Indian summer in central Wisconsin, the eastern half of Wisconsin, between Lake Michigan and Lake Winnebago, a Saturday afternoon, on the first weekend of October in 1946. It was a memorable day, not just because it was a gloriously sunny day, a one-day surprise comeback of the distant summer that most folks had forgotten. Summer was making a final appearance in a parade of gray fall days that would not relinquish their grip for quite some time, like a kid ducking in and out of the rhythmic legs of a marching band, thinking he could upset their stride.

The sun's rays felt unearthly good in the bubble of leafy, loamy, swirling autumn air that encased Carl's new red 1946 Ford Super Deluxe convertible as he and Connie road the waves of rolling pavement westward in a state of connubial bliss on Highway 151. They were headed westward out of Manitowoc on this meandering two-lane route, into the late day sun, toward Connie's hometown of Chilton.

The drive would take them past hundreds of acres of wavy, flat cornfields, but of course, the corn had been harvested. The fields lay fallow, dotted with late summer weeds beaten down by a month of morning frosts, flowing over acres and acres of colorless dirt furrows, settled in for the first blanket of snow to put them down for the winter. An early winter was in the forecast, although the farmer's didn't need to hear it from the weatherman. They knew the signs. They could tell sometimes just from that dead leaf smell of the air, but for them, clues were abundant. September's thick, dense clouds of Canadian geese had thinned noticeably in the past week. Their low altitude honking could no longer stop a conversation in mid-sentence. The migration wasn't over, but it was down to single v formations, one after another, unlike the previous weeks that had a v on top of a v on top of a v, with so many layers of v formations that the sun strobed with their passage.

Something fiercely cold was coming, and the birds knew it, although all it took, really, was a farmer's glance at the tree lines beyond the fields to see that most of the leaves were already gone, their glorious days of color but a memory. They had been knocked off their branches by cold streams of air flowing out of the Canadian tundra far to the north. Winter was coming to Wisconsin early, and it would be big.

Connie and Carl drove by the stark fields with the ragtop down, soaking in the warmth of the late afternoon sunshine and feeling a sense of inner peace that only comes from being with a person one is deeply in love with and whose love is infused with an indescribable contentment from knowing that it is mutual. They were a sublimely happy couple.

They glanced at each other every few miles, smiling and looking into each other's eyes with the same feeling they'd had for each other when they'd walked up the aisle and out of the church on the day they'd gotten married seven months and three days ago at St. Mary's Catholic Church in Chilton. Their love for each other was so intense that it could have lit all the lighthouses on both coasts of the country and all over the Great Lakes. They didn't need the sunshine of an Indian Summer day to feel warm as long as they were in each other's company, but even so, the afternoon rays felt awfully good on their faces, making them feel even more alive and carefree and a little toasty as they drove with their faces slightly turned up to confront the late afternoon sun face to face. Carl had the heater on low, further adding to their collective sense of wellbeing and mutual warmth. It was a perfectly beautiful afternoon, and Connie and Carl were a perfectly beautiful couple, perfectly in love. Every once in a while Carl would accelerate out of their casual cruising and briefly take the car up to seventy miles an hour on a straightaway, adding to the exhilaration both felt in this particular moment in their lives.

What are the words that describe the indescribable depth of love that can exist between two people? The two words "true love" serve merely as punctuation for this feeling so great, so deep, so uniquely human. That it's an indescribable love does not mean it accepts a loss for words, but simply that words are inadequate. The shortfall doesn't mean something must be able to define it, for all words are inadequate. Some know this love firsthand; others who may not, undeniably recognize it when they see it in others. It is a golden vibration that stirs every human being, and its emanations invigorate the muse in every poet's heart. Couples that have it, glow in the core of its symbiotic radiance.

This love is not elusive, even though poets often say it is. It is not even rare or as uncommon as the world's greatest romances. It happens all the time, and it is not only all around us, but deep within us as well, like a perfect seed, still and waiting but for the right combination of nutrients. When couples have it, that indescribable love, everyone else is a credible witness. It's the love that is there for everyone, a love that every human is capable of experiencing, the love that every human desires because it is what makes us human more than any other emotion. This indescribable love between two people is what it is, and it is worth hoping that it comes into our lives. But I digress.

CHAPTER FOUR

Connie and Carl, names flowing with the allure of alliteration, were silent in their drive to Chilton, taking it all in. Connie was thinking about how fast her life had changed in such a short time. She hadn't even known Carl for a year. They'd met on a Saturday in December 1945, at a Christmas party at The Manitowoc Hotel, two weeks before Christmas Day. It was a big party, maybe five or six hundred people in all, a couple of hundred at a time, probably more with the ebb and flow of couples through the late afternoon, when the party began, and well into the evening when Artie Shaw and his Orchestra were playing. The music was as wonderful as always, but the days of the big swing bands were numbered. Glenn Miller had been killed in the war; other greats had organized and reorganized. The music world was in flux with new sounds that reflected the excitement of a revitalized America. Duke Ellington led the way, but Artie Shaw could still rip up the dance floor, and he was doing exactly that in the ballroom of The Manitowoc Hotel.

The dance floor was packed with revelers from fifty miles in every direction. The social life, especially for young people in this part of the state, was defined by the convergence of small town residents to wherever big event was taking place, and on that night, the big event was in Manitowoc. A random sampling of adults who were milling around the four open bars that were set up in the corners of the ballroom would reveal a mix of people from twenty or more different towns, including the bigger towns of Green Bay, Appleton, Fond du Lac, and Sheboygan, and maybe even a few from Milwaukee, which was nearly eighty miles away. Every small town was represented—towns named Algoma, Chilton, Plymouth, Waldo, Elkhart Lake, and Luxemburg. Caravans of friends in strings of cars fifteen—even twenty—cars deep would spill out of these small towns, merging onto the highways from county roads, destined for a night of swing with Arty Shaw and his band. Manitowoc was a relatively big town, not really much of a city, but relative to the farm towns surrounding it, you could think of it as a city. Of course, Chicago and Milwaukee were cities, making everything relative I suppose, but that night, the party at the hotel was as big as any party in any city in America.

Connie was laughing with her best friend Virginia Stranski, also a Chilton girl, not far from one of the bars at the edge of the dance floor. They had come from Chilton with two other friends for an evening of dress up, cocktailing, and dancing. Her two friends, Vy and Patty, were already on the dance floor, having been swept up by two brothers they knew, who ran their own farms near Plymouth. The brothers were sizeable, and so were their farms, and neither could dance worth a lick.

Connie and Virginia were holding a martini in one hand and a cigarette in the other, thinking that was the best way to look sophisticated. That was their notion anyway, and they couldn't stop laughing over it because neither smoked nor drank alcohol, other than a glass of wine over dinner once in a while. They wanted to dance, but not with just anyone. Part of their plan was a mutual commitment to meet someone new that night, someone that neither of them had ever seen before or heard of. They both were ready to bust out of the usual list of local boys who begged them to go out, local being just about anybody from the surrounding towns.

Connie and Virginia grew up as a couple of small town Catholic girls, and their behavior was every bit modeled by the mores of that culture. Neither had been married, of course, and both had dated some nice men, but they hadn't been in the world as much as one might think for a couple of gals who were twenty-five years old. After all, throughout their early twenties, the country had been at war with the Germans and Japanese, and nobody then had a normal social life.

Now that was all behind them, and in front of them were dozens and dozens of eligible men who were back from the war and looking to start a family. They giggled over the possibilities and realized they had both downed their martinis. With an empty glass and a cigarette that was nearly spent, the timing was right, and sure enough, two tall, good looking men walked right up to both of them and asked them to dance. Carl asked Connie, and John asked Virginia. These men were from Appleton, and the girls had no idea that within four months they would each be married to the man who walked them onto the dance floor that night—but that's what happened.

It's funny how life works, how meeting someone can put a person on an entirely new course in life—just like that, just as quick as you can snap your fingers. Go ahead, dear reader, snap your fingers. You know what I mean when I say it can happen just like that. Suddenly someone steps into your life, or you step into theirs (it works both ways), and it can mean a million different possibilities, most of which you never could have imagined.

One of Connie's best friends got married the year before. A man who worked in the government, some kind of procurement position dealing with ordering and distributing armored vehicles, proposed to Sue Ann Voss, a Chilton girl who Connie shared every class with throughout St. Mary's grade school and Chilton High. They even went to the University of Wisconsin for a couple of years together before dropping out to take factory jobs to support the war effort.

Right after the wedding, Sue Ann's husband moved them to Paris to become some kind of administrator for the Marshall Plan. Just like that! Off to Paris. Everyone exclaimed, "Paris... FRANCE!" Everyone thought: no telling what can happen to a small town girl when she gets married. Not everyone stays in town or moves to a nearby farm. Connie and Virginia knew Sue Ann, and her move really hit a homerun for the possibilities.

Life sure can be exciting, and it can change dramatically, for the worse sometimes but for the better too. One of the outcomes of the war was how it got people to pay more attention to the moment. For soldiers on the battlefield, the second at hand is all that matters. As every soldier will tell you, when shells are going off everywhere and bullets are zinging by and the noise is ear-splitting, the moment is so real and life is so alive that paying attention to the moment is all you can do. And it's the only way that hope can be sustained. But I digress.

CHAPTER FIVE

Chilton was one of the small towns in that part of eastern central Wisconsin. It was a farm town surrounded by other farm towns—towns named Kiel, New Holstein, and Hilbert, among others. New Holstein was the closest town, about six miles away. The big businesses in Chilton were the K&T feed company and the canning factory, which did a lot of peas. Wisconsin wasn't just corn, you know.

Connie grew up on Main Street in Chilton, about ten blocks from the canning factory. This may not sound like much in the way of news, but the location was a boon for the kids who grew up on that street. You see, most of the farm trucks would travel down Main to get to the canning factory at the end of the street, and when the peas were harvested in the middle of summer, truck after truck would drive by the house on the way to the factory. So laden were they with peapods still stuck to the vines that clumps of vines would fall off the trucks all the time.

It was easy pickings for a kid quick and careful enough to dash into the street to get them before a car squashed them. Sometimes the clumps were as big as a bushel's worth and always yielded the sweetest freshest pods of sweet peas anyone could ever hope for. I know this for a fact because I was one of those kids who ran into the street to get them every summer while visiting my grandparents, Connie's parents. I did just what my mom had done when she was a kid. I was the second generation of pea pickers who gorged on peas fallen off the cannery-bound trucks.

To this day, I can remember sitting on the porch with mom, discovering the joy of splitting a single fat pod lengthwise with a thumbnail, right down its dark green fibrous seam, then pulling the bright green halves open and marveling at the perfectly round peas that were not much bigger than a pencil eraser, each attached to a tiny stem. Like everyone else with an open pod in hand and the close-in promise of mouthwatering sweetness, the anticipation was keen. At that point, there was nothing left to do but run a sharp thumbnail from end to end on the inside of the pod, thereby separating every pea from its stem, and then pop them into a waiting mouth or lap or, for later, a bowl.

Not much on this earth tasted better than fresh peas off a farmer's truck. I can experience everything about that memory as if I were right there this very minute, sitting as close to her as possible without officially being in her lap. Oh yeah. Sitting on the porch steps on Main Street eating fresh, sweet peas right from the pod while waiting for the next truck to drop some more was a mighty fun way for a kid to spend a summer afternoon in Chilton, where summers could be spent in perfect innocence. Bad things just didn't happen to anyone in Chilton; it was so perfect.

Chilton was a great town to grow up in, an all-American small town; every one of the two thousand residents would have said as much. Above all, Chilton was an idyllic farm town, although it had enough commerce to have a main street that ran for almost ten blocks, lined on both sides with storefronts.

Connie's family owned the town's only movie theatre, where her mom played the piano for the silent films until the talkies took over. Connie learned to read at the silent movies before she even went to school by watching the movies with all their subtitles, over and over again. New Holstein and the other nearby towns didn't have a movie house, so this one drew crowds of movie lovers from all over. This is another reason people in these small towns knew so many people in the neighboring towns. Connie's parents also owned the livery, which took care of many of the town's carriages and a constantly increasing number of automobiles when Connie was very little. Of course by her teen years, the back half of the thirties, cars were everywhere, and horses were becoming uncommon, although not entirely out of the picture.

Even so, Chilton was a farm town because it was in the middle of farmland—rich, rich farmland, fertile and perfect for crops and perfect for dairy cows. The town's people didn't think of themselves as farmers, but they all knew farmers, of course, and farmers in that particular part of the world were pretty well off. By 1946, there were rumors floating around that some of them were even rich—really rich—but true to their German heritage, no one really talked about money or let anyone know too much about what they had. Let's say that no one was ostentatious about their wealth, farmers or not. But let there be no doubt that Wisconsin farmers had a good life working the land and didn't have trouble sending their kids to college if they wanted to. A lot of topped-off silos took care of tuition easily enough, but even so, many children stayed and built their father's farms into bigger, better, and more modern farms. Kids, like Connie, who grew up in and around Chilton and knew the Depression years firsthand, understood the value of a dollar, accepted hard work as a means to accomplish something, placed an inestimable value on faith in God, and nurtured an optimism that life would always get better, although it probably wouldn't come easily.

Beyond the neighboring towns, about twenty-five miles to the north of Chilton, was Appleton, a good sized city for Wisconsin, perched at the top of Lake Winnebago, straddling the Fox River. Appleton was a city that was built off of the surrounding paper mills and mill towns. That's where Carl grew up, the youngest of four boys in a family that owned one of the bigger pulp mills for three generations. Fond du Lac was another good sized city in Wisconsin, and it was located on the other end of Lake Winnebago, about forty miles to the south. Founded as a French fur settlement, it's French for "bottom of the lake" or "foot of the lake." Manitowoc was to the east, on Lake Michigan. The three shoreline cities formed a triangle, and Chilton pretty much fell right into the middle of that triangle. What about Oshkosh, you ask? Well, by gosh, Oshkosh was on the other side of Lake Winnebago from Chilton. I had to say that, in case you were wondering, by gosh.

Carl loved Lake Winnebago and practically lived on it one summer in his teens while he and his friends became the first kids in Appleton to water ski, which was a new sport at the time, one that was invented in Minnesota in 1922 by a couple of snow skiers. He loved the water and took to waterskiing because it appealed to the daredevil in him and helped him set himself apart from his older brothers.

Carl didn't want to be like his brothers, who planned to work for their father, the owner of one of the big paper mills. He didn't want to follow them into the family business. He had other plans—plans that actually spun out of another lake activity: ice fishing. It wasn't the fishing that Carl liked—long hours sitting in the cold hoping to pull a fish out of a hole cut in the middle of an ice hut floor had no appeal for him. Nope, not enough excitement there.

As a boy, Carl loved being out there on the winter ice because he loved the ice shacks. Their simplicity reminded him of tree houses, which he loved as well. He found himself studying the various designs of the fishing shacks through impromptu visits to them. He knocked on doors fearlessly just to get invited inside, so curious was he to see how these small buildings might be made to work better in an inhospitable environment. It was this initial exposure to understanding buildings in the context of the environment that would be the basis for his devotion to Frank Lloyd Wright's concept of organic architecture, which suggested igloos would be ideal on the frozen water in the winter, but of course, that was only one possibility. By the time he was sixteen, he wanted nothing more in life than to be an architect, a love that he told his friends arose from his time exploring the ice huts on Lake Winnebago.

Lake Winnebago is only a little bigger than Lake Tahoe. But unlike that very deep lake in California, Lake Winnebago is only twenty-one feet deep at its deepest point and averages only fifteen feet, shallow enough almost everywhere to see the bottom. With a lack of depth and currents, the lake's surface freezes quickly for a few months in the typically cold winters of Wisconsin. In very cold years, the ice is so thick that it sometimes has supported as many as five thousand cars and trucks at a time, all parked on the lake ice alongside their owners' fishing huts or going to or from them. Indeed, the lake seemed particularly shallow to water skiers when they skied over the rusting wrecks of cars and trucks that had ventured over ice that hadn't been thick enough to hold them while trying to get to and from the fishing huts on less frigid years.

Carl never lost his love for waterskiing. He didn't have much time for that, however, with the postwar rush in commerce and all the design work his architectural business was bringing in. His service in the Army Corps of Engineers in the Pacific had taught him a lot about design, structure, and construction, but he didn't like to think about the war. He preferred the memories of his childhood, particularly the last time he water skied.

It was a Saturday afternoon five years earlier, before he had enlisted. It was July 12th, the birthday of his childhood best friend, Stewart Gardner. Stewart's parents had a big house on Winnebago's northwestern shoreline on Hunter's Point Road, a cushy street in Neenah where the houses ran like a string of pearls. Carl and Stewart had been waterskiing together off their dock since their early teens. After every spin out on the lake, Carl would laugh as he recalled seeing cars, sometimes one after another, submerged under his skis. It was even possible to see hundreds of them in one day of skiing. They were often no more than shadows, like blurred images of boulders, sitting on the bottom, like miniature sunken ships, all given up by their owners, never to be retrieved. Left to rot away, all were eventually reduced to rusty skeletons on the bottom of Lake Winnebago.

The graveyard of sunken cars and trucks after thirty years of people driving them on the ice, determined to get to the best fishing address on the ice, was substantial and, according to anyone who had driven on the ice, understandable. It was a risk every fisherman was willing to take. One minute the driver would be rolling down the ice roads on the surface of the lake, feeling all safe and secure, steering a vehicle slowly across the ice, and then suddenly, in the blink of an eye, a crack and a plunk! The car would fall through the ice, gone forever. Sometimes it took the driver with it—not every driver got out of the vehicle in time and made it back to the arms of good Samaritans who were waiting for him at the edge of the hole. Most got out of the water, but some weren't lucky, plain and simple. And, by gosh, just like that, a life snuffed! It happened a lot more often than people liked to think about. Nobody wants to remember accidents that took someone's life, especially the life of a loved one. But I digress.

CHAPTER SIX

The fallow fields flowed west, right up to Chilton's town boundary then suddenly stopped at a row of modest two bedroom homes that defined the fringe of town. Connie and Carl quickly dropped their speed to a crawl, the sun still in their eyes but lower now, just off the tree tops, as they pulled into town, turned right on Park Street, and then drove a few blocks to Main Street. They coasted two more blocks to get to Ruby and Henry's home on the left, where Connie had grown up. Carl made a u-turn right after he passed the house and pulled up to the curb, centering the car on the walkway leading to the front door of the house.

Ruby was Connie's mom, a cherubic being who was loved by everyone. Henry had married Ruby a year after Connie's father had died in 1926 from a heart attack one morning while he was changing a tire on his 1925 Ford Model T Torpedo. His name was John Ortlieb. Ruby found him collapsed and surely dead, only a few minutes after she had seen him from the kitchen window, walking around the car, admiring the curved fenders and a hood that was longer than the standard Model T. This four-door convertible was a step above most of Chilton's cars, and John Ortlieb was the envy of his friends with his ragtop, but moments later all envy disappeared. Nobody would want to be in his shoes again.

Ruby, a strong woman who had seen a lot in life, could barely hold herself together long enough to ask the neighbors to carry him into the house and set him on his bed. Father O'Reilly from St. Mary's was summoned to comfort her while they waited for the truck from Keller Mortuary. Connie was only five years old at the time, seven years younger than her sister, Virginia. Both girls knelt at his bedside, one on each side of Ruby, with Connie close to the foot of the bed. Her mama was kneeling, with tears pouring down her face, her elbows on the bed, both hands on John's arm, and a rosary intertwined in the trembling fingers of both hands.

Connie was afraid to look at the stillness that was her father. Connie didn't think it really looked like him. Something was really different, but death was beyond her young grasp. She hoped no one would make her touch him; she couldn't have done that. Instead, she prayed with all her might that he was just sleeping and that God would wake him up. She was told that he was in God's hands, so maybe God would give him back. He didn't wake up, and the people from Keller's took him. Connie didn't go to the funeral. That was her last memory of her father.

When she was growing up, someone had called her memories of her father "little things," but they were big things to her; they were who he was to her, like the way he smelled when he smoked his cigars, and how his face felt scratchy against her neck when he pretended he was trying to bite her ear off, and how animated he became when he was telling funny stories at the dinner table, or when he laughed so hard that tears streamed down his cheeks. He played with her a lot when he was home. They especially liked to play outside in the warm days of spring and summer. Papa would chase her around the yard, playing monster with a funny walk, his arms outstretched while calling out loud oozy noises—all of which had been absolutely terrifying, even though nothing but hugs and kisses ever happened when he caught up with her.

Once when they were playing, she fell out of one of the apple trees in the backyard and landed right at his feet. He was telling her to reach a little farther for the apple he wanted, when suddenly a branch snapped, and she fell through a couple of the lower limbs and dropped the final five feet or so onto her back, which knocked the wind out of her little frame. Stunned and wanting to be picked up and soothed, Papa just stood over her and smiled. She waited for him to bend over, for him to pick her up and hug her. He smiled and just stood there, looking down at her, as if they were both frozen in time.

She remembered that moment so well, and always would. After a long minute, he said to her, and these are the exact words, which she never forgot: "Connie, you took a nasty fall. I'm sure it hurts. Sometimes you've got to pick yourself up, yep, and just get on with what you were doing." She stood up on her own, just as he was reminding her that he was still thinking about that apple. All those things about him weren't little things to her; those were the things that kept her father alive in her heart. She loved him dearly, of course, and would always miss him.

A little more than a year after her father had died, a man named Henry Steenport married Ruby and moved into their house. Connie had come to love Henry too because he loved her, her sister, and her mother so much. Connie was sorry that God didn't let her father come back, but He did give her Henry, who would be a good father—she just knew it. She'd call him Henry—not Dad or Papa—just Henry, like everyone else did.

He wanted it that way. Those were some of her earliest memories.

When the car pulled to a stop at the curbside, perfectly lined up with the walkway to Ruby and Henry's front door, Connie snapped out of her drift into childhood memories and collected herself. Carl honked once with a quick punch of his palm on the steering column and then jumped out of the car and ran around the frontend—he always chose the front—to get to Connie's door to open it for her. He was the perfect gentleman. By the time Connie put her foot out of the car, Ruby and Henry were coming out to greet them, smiling and waving as if they hadn't seen each other in months, when in fact, Connie and Carl had spent the last weekend with them and had slept over in the extra bedroom, the one that had been Connie and Virginia's when they were growing up.

I stayed in that second bedroom as a kid when I visited Ruby and Henry for two weeks each summer. I called them Grandma and Grandpa, and I loved them and they loved me. When I was big enough to go to the shallow creek that was the property line in the field out back, Grandpa would take me there to show me how to catch crayfish. Some were pretty big, as big as my little hand, and kind of scary because they could pinch pretty hard if I put my finger in front of a claw—enough to make me yelp.

One summer, the crayfish were especially thick. There were so many, and they were so easy to catch that I must have had at least twenty-five mason jars of water by the back steps, each holding one big crayfish or a couple of small ones. It was my private collection for the duration of my visit. I wanted to donate my collection to the Smithsonian, but Grandma made me put them back in the creek when it was time for me to leave Chilton and go back home to Milwaukee.

If you don't know how to catch a crayfish, you should. It's good to learn new things, and it's pretty easy. First, you've got to find one, of course. They're usually hiding under the shelter of a rock in a shallow, quiet pool of water or sometimes in the space between two adjacent rocks. You keep sliding one rock off another, just an inch or two at a time, searching carefully until you spot one. Then, slowly get into position, which means get right over them with a big straddle. Do it too fast, and they skitter away, spooked by the movement. But if you do it just right, they won't move. Then go slowly into the water with an open jar or a can in one hand and place it behind the chosen one so that the open end is just behind its tail. Then slowly, with the other hand, the one holding a stick, put the end of stick in front of it, right in front of its claws, right up to the tips of its antenna, which is close enough to scare it. When crayfish are scared, they try to escape by propelling themselves backwards with a couple of flips of their tail, in this case, right into the opening of your jar or can. It was easy to catch them that way.

I remember Grandpa asking me what I had learned from that, and later that same day, I told my mom what I had learned. She said that Henry had taught her the same thing when she was little. That was his way, and we both remembered the lesson: sometimes when you're afraid, it's not a good thing to back up. But I digress.

CHAPTER SEVEN

Carl helped Connie out of the car. In a fleeting thought, he told himself it felt good to stretch his long legs, but what really felt good was stepping into Ruby and Henry's world. He loved calling on them at their modest house on Main Street. They were a couple who made one believe that everything was right with the world, and a home couldn't get any homier than theirs. They were the two sweetest people he knew and were loved by everyone in town. I guess you could say they embodied everything everyone in the country ever said that was positive about small town America. Ruby and Henry were standing eagerly at the top of the porch stairs of their nondescript, traditional, single story wood-framed bungalow, a period piece going back to the turn of the century.

"Connie! Carl!" Ruby called out, unable to contain her herself as she stepped down the porch stairs and trundled down the sidewalk to Connie and Carl. Henry followed her, smiling, as the young couple engulfed his Ruby in their arms, hugging her as if they hadn't seen her in months, when it really had been just a week ago that they were all together.

An hour later, all four of them were at the dinner table in the Spartan dining room, which was decorated only by a few built-in cabinets with cut glass windows that didn't really reveal much of anything in the way of contents. But it was a nice room, with windows that revealed the early dusking of the sky through the leafless trees that towered over the house. The foursome was just nicking into a dessert of homemade apple pie topped with a scoop of vanilla ice cream. Ruby had rolled the crust out and sliced the apples only a few hours earlier so that it could be hot, right out of the oven, when it was time. She had selected the best apples from a half-barrel she had stashed under the cellar stairs for just such an occasion.

Ruby's apple pie was the best in the county, and it was what every dinner guest hoped for, for dessert. Ruby made the best pies, not just apple. Her rhubarb pie, when the rhubarb was in season, was the talk of the town. Yep, that's right, the talk of the town! Unlike people in the cities, people in small towns talked about pie, and everyone knew who made the best in town. The apple pie was heavenly too and on the table as long as the apples barreled well.

Ruby's cooking was just one of many reasons Carl and Connie loved to stop by, sometimes twice in a month. They would often stay overnight if the visit coincided with a weekend, even though they lived only twenty-five miles to the north on the east side of Appleton. That woman sure could bake!

The dinner conversation was lively. "It's looking bad for Harry and his pals," Henry said, making his opening gambit to establish politics as the next topic on the table.

After sharing all of the town's news and some of the local gossip, the discussion shifted to politics. This was an election year and mid-term in Truman's presidency. Truman was a democrat, and this election was largely seen as a referendum on Truman himself, whose approval ratings had taken a dive through the summer and fall. The controversy was over the president's handling of the postwar labor strikes. The thorniest strike was the nationwide railroad strike, which affected millions of Americans because it was a time when Americans depended on the trains for both commuter and long distance travel.

There were plenty of other issues to discuss, and farmers throughout the state knew about the ones that affected them. They knew Truman waffled horrendously on all the unpopular price controls that had been put in places in the war years to handle shortages, particularly in foodstuffs. Farmers everywhere were in an uproar about them and had even stirred up the political pot over price controls on beef, which had people all fall talking with great animation about a hamburger famine. Every farmer within miles of Chilton was on edge over Truman's actions.

Ruby was already in the kitchen cleaning up the dishes, and Connie joined her right after the first mention of politics. It was a good time for a little mother and daughter catch-up. Connie was very happy with how her marriage to Carl was going and wanted to tell her mama all about everything that had happened since last weekend, which wasn't much, but the two of them could turn a carrot into a carrot cake in no time. They could hear the men talking politics, and Carl's clear baritone voice made it through the kitchen door with particular clarity.

"Yep, you're right about that, Henry. Everyone in Appleton is thinking that this is the last administration run by democrats that we'll see in a long time."

"Well, don't count 'em out. They have two more years in Washington. A lot can happen."

"You mean changes from the heat Harry's getting?"

"Yep, you betcha," Henry answered. "Harry and his pals are still running the ship. You saw all that commotion when he lifted price controls on beef two weeks ago."

"Criminey," Carl retorted, "that shot the meat prices to record levels in a matter of days. That's all anyone's talking about now."

"And there's more of them shenanigans to happen too. Mark my words, Carl, you'll be seeing plenty of Harry's tricks right up to the election."

"Oh, I don't doubt it, Henry, but don't you think it's a little late for that? Aren't the cows already out of the barn?"

"Not with the beef prices where they are now!" Henry declared.

"With beef prices up so high right now, no cow is safe," Carl paused, "in or out of the barn!" They both laughed pretty hard at that thought.

Ruby called into the dining room, "You men ready for some coffee?"

"My usual, Ruby," Henry called, putting his order in for nothing but black.

Carl followed up, tossing his voice through the door, "Thanks, Ruby, cream and one sugar for me! I'm going to have some more sugar later… isn't that right, Connie?" He smiled at Henry and raised an eyebrow upward for a truly mischievous look.

"I heard that, Carl Koehler," Connie called from the kitchen, "and don't think you can say things like that in front of Mama and Henry!"

"So, Henry," Carl continued, "you think Senator LaFollette is going to get reelected? You know he's not a democrat. That's in his favor."

"Maybe," Henry replied. "Hard to say. He might. His father was Fightin' Bob LaFollette, so he surely has some of the same stuff in him. It don't look good, but it don't look bad neither. He's been around twenty-one years; that oughta count for something. Still, hard to say if the Progressive Party isn't in just as much hot water as the Democrats." Henry shook his head and shrugged his shoulders, making a point about not being sure of anything. "I just don't know. It's hard to say, Carl... Yep, just too hard to say."

"Yeah, hard to say, Henry, what with the Progressives not liking LaFollette right now for jumping back to the Republican party last year. You know, he is a Republican now and that's how he's running."

"I know that," Henry replied, "but I think of him as a Progressive and a lot of other people do too." Henry paused as he and Carl both looked into the kitchen, wanting, no doubt, their coffee. "Hard to make sense of him, and that don't do so much for him."

Carl nodded and craned his neck toward the kitchen.

Henry continued. "A lot of Republicans resented him when he joined the Progressives a while back. Nope, they haven't forgiven him for that, even if he did come back to the party. That McCarthy fella might take him."

"What? You think Joe McCarthy has a chance?" Carl asked, making a face like he had just tasted something sour.

Connie set their coffees in front of them and returned to the kitchen, looking at Carl for the flash of a second and shaking her head over the anticipation of a discussion about Joe McCarthy. It came up a lot lately—too much—but they had fun with it. She didn't pay any attention to Joe McCarthy. She thought he was just another big mouth in politics—maybe the biggest.

"'Course he has," Henry stated with some confidence, "and his chances are getting better every day. You wait and see. McCarthy could be our next senator."

"Yeah," Carl said, "I've been watching the polls. He's making a charge, all right."

"Yep," Henry replied, "could be U.S. Senator Joseph McCarthy, Senator Big Mouth." Henry laughed to himself, and Carl only looked partially amused.

"Hey, Connie," Carl called out toward the kitchen, "you hear that? Henry thinks your ol' pal Joe McCarthy is going to be United States Senator Joe McCarthy!"

Connie stuck her head into the dining room while leaning up against the doorframe, her feet planted squarely in the kitchen. "Oh Carl, you stop that nonsense immediately. Joe McCarthy is not my ol' pal and never was."

"You could have been a Senator's wife... Connie McCarthy—no make that Mrs. Joe McCarthy." Carl was leaning back in his chair, looking up at the ceiling, half-smiling, and enjoying what he thought was a little harmless ribbing.

"Carl Koehler, you stop saying that silliness right away," Connie called from the kitchen. "You know I never had a date with him, and I was never interested in him, the big blowhard. I don't even like thinking about him."

Carl wouldn't let up. He was enjoying this too much. "Well he proposed to you, didn't he?"

"He certainly did not! And you know that!"

"He called you up from all over Wisconsin two years ago, didn't he? He was hound-doggin' you, honey!"

Connie turned her head into the kitchen and laughed, "Mama, make Carl stop saying those awful things about me and Joe McCarthy."

"Carl," Ruby retorted, "you are something! Do you have to tease Connie every time Joe McCarthy's name comes up?"

Before Ruby could admonish him any further, Carl couldn't resist his little fun with his beautiful wife. "Well, he did, didn't he? Wasn't he calling you all the time? And sending roses?"

Connie looked back in the kitchen again, and then she looked at Henry, who was now glancing back at her, although his back was pretty much to the kitchen door, fully into the conversation, maybe even enjoying it a little bit. Not much could fluster Connie, but this subject got her a little red-faced. "Henry, you too, you tell Carl to stop this. It isn't right to talk like that."

With no help from Ruby or Henry, Connie realized that she would have to defend herself. "Carl, you know I've told you plenty of times that there was never anything there. He called a couple of times, but I wouldn't give him the time of day. I told you I was never interested in that man."

"And roses?" Carl teased some more.

Absentmindedly and with little expression, Connie confessed, "He sent me roses a couple of times and even asked me out, but I never had any interest in that man. He was so uncouth." Connie said "uncouth" as if it were the nastiest word she could think of. On the heels of her emphatic derision, she stammered, "Why, why…, you know, Carl, I think he's revolting!" Ruby slipped past her to refill the empty cups of coffee. "Besides, he's way too old for me," Connie continued, regaining her composure and looking directly at Carl. Her tone softened. "Carl you know you're the only man I have ever loved. And you're the only man I ever will love! Now drink your coffee while I finish up in the kitchen with Mama."

On that note, Connie returned to the kitchen sink to dry the last few dishes and enjoy the exclusive company of her mother once more. She closed the swinging door just to make sure they didn't have to hear anymore of all that talk about politics that was coming out of the dining room.

Just as the door stopped gyrating, Connie heard Carl call out. "Connie… Connie?"

She and Ruby stopped passing dishes and stood in silent suspense for whatever was next.

"Connie," Carl said in what sounded like a light and playful voice, "just so you know… you're the only woman I have ever loved and ever will, no matter what!"

The dishes were passed again, with washing and drying in syncopated harmony once again, this time with big smiles on Ruby and Connie's faces. Ruby looked at Connie with all the love a mother can feel for her daughter and whispered, "He's a keeper, Connie… but the dickens!"

Connie was sure that Carl was the only man she'd ever love. She couldn't imagine finding any room in her heart for anyone but Carl or, for that matter, ever living without him. Her heart was his—he could have it all—and she couldn't possibly conceive of any other love for a man than the love she felt for Carl and would always feel for him.

Love, as I said earlier, is a fragile thing, and like a flame, it can be easily extinguished. But, with the right person, it can also be enduring, so enduring that it outlasts every other emotion. Love endures. It can live in our hearts forever, and it was to be in Connie's and Carl's hearts forever. It is as simple as that.

Joe McCarthy was not the right person for Connie; Carl was. Joe McCarthy, dear reader, as you may know, won the election to the U.S. Senate in 1946, surprising almost everyone with his victory over LaFollette. His first four years were undistinguished in every way, but in 1950, he moved into the forefront of the national stage with a speech asserting that he had a list of hundreds of members of the Communist Party and members of a spy ring, all of which were employed by the State Department. He also attacked private citizens throughout the country, also accusing them of ties with the Communist Party.

Eventually, Joe McCarthy brought disgrace upon himself and tarnished the reputation of government. In 1954, the Senate censored him, and his disgrace became complete. The Senate declared his behavior "inexcusable," "reprehensible," and "vulgar and insulting." He died at age forty-eight in 1957 of hepatitis. Not many mourned him, for he had wreaked havoc in American society and wrecked the lives of many falsely accused citizens. He inspired no one. But I digress.

CHAPTER EIGHT

Three hours after their arrival in Chilton and a half hour after dinner with Ruby and Henry, Carl and Connie climbed into their car for the drive home to their place in Appleton, just twenty-five miles to the north, right up Highway 57 to the town of Forest Junction, then west for fifteen miles to their home. The cold air settled on the ground the instant the sun went down and left no doubt that winter would make a good run of it in Wisconsin that year.

Before they pulled off the curb, Carl had the convertible top up, but the windows were down on Connie's side so that they could yell out their goodbyes to Ruby and Henry, who stood just ten feet back. A couple of minutes later, they were pulling out of town with Carl accelerating to sixty as quickly as possible to get the full flow of hot air coming through the vents. Within five minutes, the heater was running on full fan and maximum heat, which made for a very toasty ride home. Forty-five minutes after waving goodbye to Ruby and Henry, Carl dropped Connie off in front of their apartment building on Drew Street and then drove around to the back of the building to put the car into the garage for the night.

It was a peaceful, tree-lined neighborhood, only a few blocks north of the Lawrence College campus, at the edge of the Fox River. Mostly made up of big old Victorian homes, there were a couple of small apartment buildings and corner mom and pop grocery stores scattered within a twenty-block area. None of the apartment buildings had any more than eight apartments.

Carl and Connie's two-story building was one of the biggest commercial buildings, with its eight apartments, and theirs was in the northeast corner of the second floor, overlooking the small, grassy yard that separated the building from a garage that was sectioned off into eight stalls. This time of the year, the grass had already been killed off by the frost, and there were very few leaves sitting on the ground. Most had been raked every weekend by the building's only maintenance man, a college student named Earl, who lived in a room in the basement and got a warm place to stay in exchange for keeping up the property.

With the car parked for the night, Carl bounded up the back steps two at a time and entered their apartment through the backdoor, which opened into their kitchen. The door was unlocked. Connie had already unlocked it, turned the heat up, and was waiting for him in their bedroom—exactly where he wanted her to be. They were in bed together within minutes of Carl's entry, but it wasn't sleep they had on their minds; that would come later.

Thirty minutes later, after a frenzy of turning and rolling and more turning, with arms and legs entwined in uncountable ways, punctuated with grunting, humming, heavy breathing, and laughter too, and exhaustion from a fun and passionate round of lovemaking, Carl and Connie, naked, lay still, like spoons, herself engulfed in Carl's big, strong arms. Carl's head was bent forward, slightly behind hers, putting his lips behind her ear and losing them in her long, flowing, disheveled, blonde hair. He maximized his coverage of her body, his arms around her, coming together in front of her, encasing her arms and folded over her breasts, his legs entwined with hers, making himself perfectly aligned with her entire body, creating between them as much contact from head to toe as two bodies could have. It was perfect architecture. They lay still, connected, sharing the perfection of the moment, warm and secure, under a goose down comforter, which trapped the intensity of their closeness.

"Whatcha thinking, baby?" Carl whispered softly behind Connie's ear.

She didn't respond. She couldn't, so silent in her contentment and love for him.

"You're thinking how much I love you… aren't you?" His voice was barely audible as he sent the warmth of his breath around her ear, increasing her indescribable sense of wellbeing.

She nodded once, barely, but enough to be an answer, as a tear of joy welled up in each eye.

"I do, you know," Carl softly whispered, very softly, aware that his lips were brushing the rim of her ear. "I love you very much." He paused, knowing that she was listening. "You're my everything." He paused again. "You're all that matters to me."

She nodded again, once, but it was enough to communicate that she understood him. A tear broke free and trickled to the side of her nose and then stopped. It was the only movement in the room, that and the pounding of their hearts. She was tuned into Carl's heart, his chest pressed up against her back. It was so strong, so steady. It pulsed as if it were inside of her. He felt so vital and so powerful. For her, this was as good as life gets. A chill ran down her spine, and her body tingled as Carl's lips moved along her ear again, his warm breath washing over it and across her cheek. She loved the way he smelled when they were close like this, like the musky sweetness of an old cotton shirt that had been worn a couple of times in the forest, almost earthy, but fresh and clean like a warm current of morning air. Nothing else meant anything in these moments of infinite intimacy.

He whispered again, "I love you, baby," and then he hummed softly in her ear, "mmmm mmmm mmmmmmmmm," like he does right after he puts his nose up to Ruby's freshly baked bread and inhales its delicious warmth and contemplates its promise of perfection.

His lips tickled her ear a bit, a sensation that created a slight smile on her lips. "How," Connie thought to herself, "could she be so lucky to have a man love her so, a man she loved so much?" She pondered this mystery for a fleeting second and sighed, thinking about how perfect life can be. And then she closed her eyes and surrendered to sleep. Carl fell asleep too, with his Connie in his arms. They would sleep like that, together, for hours and then in the morning come together again.

There's no feeling like the feeling of being in love. It fills the cup of life with contents so luscious and divine that we never forget their taste, contents that are heavenly and sweet on the lips from the start, carrying the promise of immeasurable warmth and joy. And the best part about it is that when you're in love, the cup is never empty, no matter how much of its contents are consumed. But I digress.

CHAPTER NINE

Later that morning, a couple of hours after Carl had left the apartment on a mission of errands and a little catch-up on some work at his office, Connie went to the bedroom to lie down. She needed a nap; it had been a busy weekend. As she lay in the silence of the curtained room, she wasn't thinking about anything in particular, just dozing into some quiet place in her mind, when everything went still, and suddenly she knew she was pregnant. It occurred to her that it had happened last night, maybe in the morning, but she knew. Something deep inside her was different. Her inner voice asked, "Could it be?" and in the same breath, a soft, barely discernible smile formed on her lips as she answered her own question. She was pregnant and would wait and see before saying anything to anyone. There was no better secret, and when the time came to tell Carl, she could say that dreams come true. More than anything in her life, she wanted to be a mother.

There are women who know within hours after the divine act that they are pregnant. Not all, but some women, for some reason, just know. Maybe they actually feel a physical change brought on by the onset of maternal hormones or simply experience a glow of warmth or a tingle where there was none before. It's indescribable really, other than the common ground of just knowing. Maybe it's a flicker of some primordial light or a subtle change in the internal drift of intuition or a whisper from some dormant chamber in a woman's soul. Whatever it is, if the host is in a singular moment of peace and serenity, that may be the best time for knowing things that are otherwise lost in the hustle and bustle of living life, a life that exists in ourselves at so many different levels of consciousness. But I digress.

CHAPTER TEN

A couple of months passed. A nasty winter was underway, the one that everyone had predicted. It arrived earlier than usual, just as the farmers knew it would, and didn't let go. It delivered its first snowfall in mid-October and several more week after week. It was a Halloween that the trick or treaters would never forget; every one of them was bundled up, with their costumes buried under layers of sweaters, which were encased under heavy woolen coats, which were knotted at the collar with woolen scarves to seal the heat in and protect young, vulnerable necks.

The snow wouldn't melt; instead, it layered up through Thanksgiving and into December, with a fresh snowfall every week. No one was dreaming of a white Christmas; they were dreaming of just getting through the winter—a winter that hadn't even hit the midway point. The prospect of five more months of snow actually scared a lot of people, especially the farmers. It could mean bad flooding in the spring. Snow was everywhere, piled high alongside every driveway and roadway, sometimes as high as twelve feet. The snow had become burdensome, although few could resent the crystalline beauty brought on by each new snowfall.

Carl returned to their apartment after stepping out for ten minutes. He left to get the car out of the garage and drive it to the front curb, where it was parked with the engine idling so that he could have the heat on and ready for their departure. Earl had kept the sidewalk clear of snow, making for a nice path from the building's front door to the car. "Connie will like that," he thought to himself, as he stepped up on to the walkway leading to the building's front door. His breath vaporized around his head as he walked up the sidewalk to enter the building. The sun had set, and the beastly cold already had its claws out.

Carl stood in the center of the open door of their apartment, impatiently waiting for Connie. His tall, manly stature nearly filled the doorway, his coat on and a fedora perched on his head, its peak not far below the lintel of their door. He was looking rakishly handsome and ready to get the evening started. His love for her was measureless, and at this moment, it was palpable. He felt as he had often felt, like he could be content in life doing nothing more than holding her in his arms, but at the moment, they were running late for a big Christmas party forty miles away.

It was a big bash, all the way down in Fond du Lac, which was at the other end of Lake Winnebago. Big. Carl and Connie had spent many hours spreading the word among their friends. This party, to be held at a popular roadhouse just north of the town, quickly became the Christmas party of the season for their broad circle of friends, many of whom had been at their wedding the previous March. Connie and Carl loved their friends, and their friends loved them. They were the "it" couple, with endearing personalities and an entourage of friends that made them so alluring that everyone wanted to be around them.

Carl was tall, broad-shouldered, and handsome, with a charismatic presence that stopped every conversation when he entered a room, and Connie was very beautiful, although not in a big-city, stylish way. Hers was a natural, wholesome beauty that captivated every man who had ever looked into her golden hazel eyes.

They were a fun couple and laughed a lot in each other's company. Carl had a terrific sense of humor and engaged everyone who came in contact with him. If there was anyone in a room that he didn't know, you could bet he would befriend that person. Everyone said he was a great conversationalist, but if you asked Carl what made him that way, he'd kind of shuck it off and say, "All I do is ask people questions about themselves."

Carl and Connie radiated warmth and had looked forward to this party all month. It was a chance to be with friends, many of whom they hadn't seen since their wedding, and there wasn't anything they liked more than being with dear friends. They loved their friends almost as much as they loved each other.

Carl, framed in the doorway, called into the apartment gently, in a sing-song voice, projecting his smooth baritone voice across their living room and down the hallway through the open bedroom door. "Connie... I'm missing you. We have to go, sweetheart!"

"Coming Carl... be there in a minute!" she called out, in a voice so loving that Carl's impatience melted and was replaced by the anticipation of seeing his beautiful wife all dressed up for the evening.

A minute later, Connie floated out the hallway and across the living room, dressed in a black cocktail gown with long sequined sleeves and high heels that would make them the tallest couple at the party. She was radiant.

Connie opened the closet door and reached in for her coat. "You know, Carl," she said, smiling and looking beguiling, "tomorrow will make it one year since we met."

Carl stepped into the room and helped her with her coat. "Yep," he said, "December fifteenth last year at The Manitowoc Hotel—a day that will live in infamy." He laughed at his words, which mimicked Roosevelt's statement just after the Japanese viciously bombed Pearl Harbor. Connie ignored it. He slipped her coat up her awaiting arms and stepped into her back, putting his arms around her from behind. He leaned forward, his lips moved to her cheek, and whispered, "I remember... I saw you at the edge of the dance floor, and you took my breath away," and then started nibbling at her ear, "and you still do, baby."

"Carl, stop that! You're messing up my hair." She wriggled free of him.

He stepped into the open doorway again, placing one foot into the hallway, and turned to look at Connie, as she paused at the mirror that was built into the antique coat caddy just off the front door to look into it for one last double check of her makeup and to assure herself that her lipstick was perfect.

Carl looked at her adoringly as she leaned toward the mirror and pushed a strand of hair from one perfect location to another.

It was at that very moment, the moment that Connie altered the placement of a few strands of her blonde hair, when her eyes locked into the eyes of the image staring back at her in the mirror, her image. The image had an intensity she wasn't feeling, and suddenly it spoke to her, although her own face remained perfectly still. It said, "You will never see me again."

Carl saw her face unexpectedly register a momentary and entirely unexpected look of shock, as she froze, perfectly motionless, in front of the mirror. "What is it, sweetie? Are you all right?" he asked, perplexed and concerned because obviously something just happened to her. And then whatever had induced that inexplicable look on her face passed as quickly as it had appeared.

Connie said nothing, letting several seconds pass. She had no explanation for what had just happened to her and wasn't sure it had even happened. The words from her reflection certainly didn't make any sense to her. She regained her composure and turned to Carl, who was standing four feet away, waiting for her. "It's nothing, Carl," she said, excising that most strange occurrence out of her mind as nonchalantly as plucking a strand of fallen hair from her shoulder.

She turned from Carl and glanced into the mirror again, seeing nothing but the beautiful face of a young woman radiating happiness because she was going to a party with the man she loved. "Come on, honey, let's go or we'll be late!" With those words, they walked into the hallway, locked the door behind them, and officially began their evening out. It was Saturday, December 14, 1946. It was only until sometime later that she came to understand the meaning of those words that had come from the mirror.

Of course, no one knows what the future holds or even what's in store in the next few hours. It's that way for everyone, but few of us think like that and certainly fewer live like that. It makes sense to plan for things and, in fact, it's necessary. As for looking back, well, no one can deny that it's fun to recall the good times with a little reminiscing. Nonetheless, focusing on the present moment makes that moment even more alive and, consequently, more memorable when we do recall it later. Life is a collection of stories and remembrances, and the best way to have them to draw upon in the future is to be as present in the moment as possible. But I digress.

CHAPTER ELEVEN

When Connie and Carl left Appleton behind them, they were on Highway 41 heading south, down the western side of Lake Winnebago. About halfway in their journey to Fond du Lac, they would bypass the city of Oshkosh. The drive was roughly forty miles in all, in the dark the whole way, of course, since the sun had set over an hour ago. It would be an easy drive and relatively smooth, thanks in part to the recent paving of the highway. Highway 41 was a major artery in central Wisconsin and rarely cut through the hamlets of these farmlands.

The traffic was expected to be light, since the cold weather kept a lot of people from going out this time of year. The heater in Carl's car was up to the task, but it would be on high the whole way, since the temperature was dropping hourly; and it was, after all, a convertible, although the top was up, of course. The temperature was expected to fall into the teens that night, and it was already in the mid-twenties.

It was a clear sky, an open sky, over Wisconsin that night, and anyone who bothered to look up would be given the gift of a million stars. There really weren't any big cities in central Wisconsin, and the lights from Oshkosh and the surrounding small towns didn't create enough diffused light to knock out any stars. Without a blanket of clouds, the earth's inhabitants in that part of the world were going to get colder that night, no doubt about that, but in exchange, nature gave them a truly spectacular view of the celestial constellations overhead.

The drive back would be different—a lot different— because they wouldn't be driving all the way back to Appleton at a late hour. Instead, they'd told Ruby and Henry that they'd finish out the weekend with them. They loved their time together, and waking up to one of Ruby's Sunday breakfasts was something they did about once a month. Ruby loved to pamper them, which was just fine with Connie and Carl. They had told Ruby and Henry not to wait up because it would be a late night and, also, not to worry.

This meant that the return trip would take them up the eastern side of Lake Winnebago, and it would be only a twenty-minute drive from Fond du Lac to Chilton, which was half the distance to Appleton. They would drive home Sunday afternoon after a lazy morning of eating and lounging with Ruby and Henry.

The party was at Schrinsky's, a popular roadhouse on the east side of Fond du Lac on Highway 23. Club S, as the locals called it, was known for its dual reputation of offering great steak dinners and having a well-stocked late night bar. The other nice thing about Schrinsky's was its party room in the back. That's the room where the gang would meet. This party had been arranged by six guys in Carl's vast circle of friends. They had lined up "The Destinations," a really popular band in the area, to make it happen on the dance floor, and had set up a few holiday decorations, all funded by the two bucks they would charge each couple at the entrance. The turn-out in the first hour after the official start time assured them that this party would be a money-making proposition.

Connie and Carl pulled in just before eight o'clock. The

gravel in the parking lot was united in a layer of ice, making it easy for the hundred-plus cars to maneuver into whatever parking space could be claimed without worrying about the slip and slide that mud and slush create in most unpaved lots in warmer times. Carl dropped Connie off at the brightly-lit side entrance to save her the walk, and hunted down a space. The big Schlitz sign over the door illuminated the entire parking lot. No one was standing outside, which was often the case on warm summer nights, but not on this night; the biting cold made sure of that.

Connie took a few steps inside the door and would wait on the threshold for Carl. She could have gone into the building to her friends, but she waited for Carl. She liked to walk into rooms on his arm. He made her feel like royalty, and it often gave her a flashback of the walk to the throne she had made at Chilton High School when she was the Homecoming Queen nearly eight years ago. Life felt special on Carl's arm—that's just the way it was for her.

She scanned the party room from the foyer. It was quite a party and clearly well underway. The joint was jumping, and Connie immediately spied a dozen of her close friends and waved back to them. Carl stepped in moments later, paid the cover charge, whispered something to her about her coat, helped her with it, shucked his, and stepped over to the coat-check closet. Thankfully, it was being managed by someone, a girl who looked like she might be in high school. She called him "sir" and took their coats, following his instructions to hang them in a distant corner, out of the way of all the jostling and stuffing of even more coats that would probably come later, which was sure to swell the mass of wool and fur to pressing proportions.

Carl took Connie's arm and, together, they ventured into the swirling currents of their friends, where everyone had a drink in hand and offered a flurry of greetings and shout outs that wouldn't slow down for twenty minutes. Connie heard a couple of people yell out, "Connie and Carl are here!" as she got swept into the euphoria of hugging and air kissing dozens of friends that converged on the two of them. Carl was busy shaking hand after hand. Everyone around them was calling out "Merry Christmas!" It was, after all, the season, and Carl and Connie shared their joy in seeing so many friends. He was glowing, she could tell, from the excitement and pleasure of being in the midst of it all. Within a minute, her arm was free from his as he was engulfed by his buddies, and she, too, was surrounded by her girlfriends. The party was on!

Within an hour, the party room was standing room only. The room was warm, and the dance floor was hot. Bodies bumped and twirled, and glasses clinked, with their icy contents swirling, and gaiety filled the room more than the smoke from the cigarettes that rested in almost every hand on the perimeter of the dance floor. Everywhere laughter rose and fell like a rollercoaster, abundant on the heels of countless stories and pure exuberance for life.

The exhilaration over expectations arising from the ripening peacetime was unrestrained, dreams and hopes were boundless, and you could hear this in every conversation. There was a cacophony of optimism spewing out of every voice. Party plans were made, deals went down, and careers switched to another track, always with a bigger and bigger promise for the future, one that never looked so bright. Club S was a happening place, and everyone would have said the same thing: it seemed that everything was right and nothing could go wrong. The band played on and on, and they played all the hits right up to midnight, including the ones made famous by the greats like Johnny Mercer, Nat King Cole and, of course, Frank Sinatra.

That party at Schrinsky's was what everyone recalled years later as the perfect Christmas party, loaded with lighthearted party revelers who danced and danced and danced. For at least three couples, it was the tipping point that moved them into marriage. And, for everyone, it was an evening that captured the collective joy shared by friends, a joy that was accentuated with every note from the band and rose and rose with the delirium of the beat and rhythm of the room to an escalation that made time fly, as it always does when you're having fun.

In a way, it's a shame that time flies when you're having so much fun. It's such an injustice. It makes the good times so fleeting and in such stark contrast to the bad times, those times we all know to varying degrees, when it seems like the clock stops and you'll never get through the boredom, out of the doldrums, or—worse—through something painful, if that be your fate. Pain can make temporary seem like forever. But I digress.

CHAPTER TWELVE

Connie and Carl left Club S just after midnight. The party was still going strong, but they were never the ones to close a place down. Besides, Connie was tired and, as much fun as the evening had been, she was ready to call it a night. They were also mindful of the drive ahead of them. It wasn't a terribly long drive to Ruby and Henry's, but it wasn't just down the street either. It was about twenty miles north on State Road 55, which ran up the eastern shore of Lake Winnebago, and then almost ten more going east on country road 151, in the middle of a brutally cold winter night. All she wanted to do at this point was climb into a warm bed with Carl and snuggle into a deep sleep.

Carl had had one Manhattan on the rocks at Club S. That was the only cocktail he ever ordered, and he never had more than one when he was out. Connie ordered one too, but rejected it as soon as she took the first sip. Alcohol generally wasn't her thing; it didn't sit well with her. She just never could get the hang of it and pretty much accepted the reality that she just didn't like the taste of liquor.

Even rum and Coke didn't sit well with her that night, which was the drink of choice among her girlfriends. Just before midnight at Club S, she took a sip from Londa Gardner's drink, a rum and Coke that was mostly rum, and handed it back. It tasted worse than she had remembered, and this made her think that her pregnancy might be accentuating this distaste.

That's right—Connie was indeed pregnant, almost three months into it. Two weeks ago her doctor had said it might be a little premature to tell anyone until she got a little closer to three months, warning her that miscarriages happen a lot more often than people realize. She heeded his cautionary counsel, although the excitement of the possibility of a newborn was barely containable. She so badly wanted to tell Carl—and Mama too. She hadn't told anyone yet and was waiting for the right moment—maybe tomorrow over breakfast at Mama and Henry's would be the right moment. She smiled to herself at the idea and folded her hands over her tummy, feeling warm and wonderful over the idea that she and Carl were going to have a baby.

In the first fifteen miles of the drive out of Fond du Lac, Connie and Carl filled each other in on all the news they had picked up about their friends: the new jobs and the moves that came with them, the new businesses, the engagements and weddings that would be coming up, and the babies on the way. Carl was so excited when he learned that their friends, Stewart and Londa, were expecting their first child in the summer. Stew was his oldest friend and, like Carl, had gotten married the first year after the war. He was clearly happy for Stew and Londa.

Carl had expressed his hope to Connie that they would have children too and, a few times, he'd said he hoped it would be soon. From the start, they both had talked about their hopes and dreams for a family, and now their first was on the way. Connie bit down on her lower lip. She wanted to tell him so badly right then about her pregnancy, but she was determined to wait till the morning, which she felt would be the perfect time and place to make her announcement.

A couple of miles before the turnoff, their conversation had given way to silence. Connie was tired, perhaps because she was carrying. The blackness of all the whiteness that surrounded them in the darkness outside was overwhelming, and everything was lost in the darkness except for what the headlights picked up in their forward-looking vectors of light. Connie closed her eyes in contentment, with an inner happiness that she felt to the very core of her being. For an instant she recalled her distaste for Londa's rum and Coke earlier that night, having taken barely a sip, and then drifted back to another memory, one from college, when she and Virginia Stranski had shared a bottle of whiskey at a fraternity party their freshman year at the University of Wisconsin—that's right, an entire bottle.

Connie and Virginia were chatting with a guy in his frat room when he handed a bottle of Jack Daniels to Virginia and told her to open it. Then he stepped out of the room for some reason. Connie and Virginia looked at each other and shrugged and smiled over getting the same idea of taking a slug right out of the bottle of Jack Daniels—why not, they agreed, it might liven the party up a little.

The first swallow burned their throats, but they laughed, hysterically in wheezes, gasping for air and fighting the sudden flush of tears pouring out of their eyes. One more surely would be better, a thought that had occurred to both of them simultaneously, as they began laughing over the agreeability of that thought. The next swallow wasn't so bad and, given the view out the window—a view that screamed winter, a view of ice-covered Lake Mendota through the bare trees on that moonlit night—the bottled heat warmed them up a bit, so they told themselves. They passed the bottle back and forth, not recalling at a later date if they had emptied it or not, although they were told a day later that there was indeed an empty Jack Daniels bottle not far from their feet, where they sat, leaning against each other, side by side, with their backs propped against a bed, like two rag dolls, out cold.

It was just one event at a wild party at the Phi Gamma Delta fraternity house on Langdon Street that fall. The Badgers had upset the Michigan State football team that afternoon, or one of the Big Ten teams—Connie couldn't recall exactly which one—so the campus was loud and boisterous that night with happy alums and victory-crazed students. But it was the liquor that made the weekend particularly memorable for Connie and Virginia—or should I say *not* memorable? How they made it back to their rooms at Chadbourne Hall that night would forever remain a mystery, but they sure were sick in the very early hours of the morning and throughout the next day. As a consequence of that regrettable adventure into a bottle of Jack in some Fiji's room, they both lost interest in liquor.

Carl was quiet, his eyes focused on the road. He knew it was about two more miles before the turnoff to Chilton. He was lost in thought and peering steadily forward into the limited blackness in front of him, the one defined only by his headlights. He was thinking of the limitless opportunities the future held for the two of them. He was content, and his happiness had been evident to everyone at Club S. It showed in his face. It showed in how he carried himself, just a little taller on his already tall frame. And it showed in his tone of voice. Carl personified optimism, and every one of his friends shared his excitement for the future. It was difficult for him to say goodnight to their friends; they all loved each other in that special way that defines true friendships.

He now felt so complete and so confident in his life, and the difference, he knew, was that he had a wonderful woman in his life, one who loved him every minute, unconditionally. It was a love like no other in his life, and Connie was like no other woman he had ever known. He was surprised that his eyes watered just then, just for a moment, being so overwhelmed with his love for her. He turned to look at her, her head tilted, resting against her side window while she stared into the blackness, lost in her own thoughts.

Oh, in case you didn't know, a member of the Phi Gamma Delta fraternity is a called a Fiji. The nickname Fiji was born at New York University and adopted in the national fraternity in 1894 in the belief that the term would be memorable and appeal to the imagination in all things applicable to Phi Gamma Delta. It is frequently used because the fraternity's Greek letters are considered sacred by its members and are never to be displayed on any object that can be easily destroyed. This I know, dear reader, because I was once a Fiji—and I guess I still am, since members are brothers for life. That is one of the tenets of the fraternity, stated in the fraternity's charter. In a way, all references to Fiji speak to the impermanence of so many things in life. It makes one come to realize that there are few things in this world that cannot be destroyed. But I digress.

CHAPTER THIRTEEN

The song that Doris Day took to the top of the charts in 1944:

> Gonna take a sentimental journey,
> Gonna set my heart at ease.
> Gonna make a sentimental journey,
> to renew old memories.
>
> Got my bags, got my reservations,
> Spent each dime I could afford.
> Like a child in wild anticipation,
> I Long to hear that, "All aboard!"
>
> Seven... that's the time we leave at seven.
> I'll be waitin' up at heaven,
> Countin' every mile of railroad
> track, that takes me back.
>
> Never thought my heart could be so yearny.
> Why did I decide to roam?
> Gotta take that sentimental journey,
> Sentimental journey home.
> Sentimental journey.

The radio in the dashboard of Bill Jankowicz's long haul truck was turned all the way up. He loved his truck, a 1945 K Model International. It was a two-ton big rig, running on six wheels with four-wheel drive, and carried whatever could fit into the seventeen feet of the attached free-floating closed trailer.

Doris Day was coming in loud and clear singing "Sentimental Journey" with the Les Brown Band. Recorded in 1944, it stayed at the top of the charts for a long time. It was still a favorite in December, 1946. It was one of Bill Jankowicz's favorite songs. He knew all the lyrics—everybody did—and he often sang it when he was driving, even when the radio was off, but it was sure a lot better when he could sing along.

He had pulled out of the old battered barn behind his house in Stockbridge ten minutes earlier and was now driving south on State Road 55, just passing through the hamlet of Quinney, heading for Fond du Lac, when the tune came on. He thought it was a good omen to hear that song, especially at the start of his journey. He was a sentimental man and a family man and just liked singing the word *sentimental* over and over again. It sat well with him, although he wasn't much for roaming but preferred to be at home with his wife and newly minted teenage son Billy Jr.

Bill was an independent trucker and, as such, his work required travel. Fortunately for him, the pay was so good that it made it easier for him to take the time away. This would be a good trip: it was a double load, something to haul to Denver, where he'd unload and then pick up something else and bring it back to Chicago. He could be back home in six days if everything went smoothly.

He had to load up in Chicago at six that morning. Leaving his place in Stockbridge a few minutes after midnight would give him plenty of time to get there for his early morning pick-up. He wanted to get onto Highway 41 going south out of Fond du Lac for a straight shot to Chicago, not quite a half hour from where he was.

Within the first ten minutes of his ride, in the darkest hours of this very dark night, Bill was thinking about the weather. For the night, it looked pretty good for trucking, despite the freezing temperatures. He had a good heater in his cab, and the windbreak covering his grill would help keep the heat under the hood stable. No blizzards were in the forecast into the week. All in all, it was looking like a pretty tame week for snowfalls—maybe it would be the first week in a month without snow, although it was a hard call to make with all the open space ahead of him in Iowa and Nebraska.

For now, the roads were dry and, for a change, free of ice, especially on the more heavily traveled roads in central Wisconsin. However, he didn't assume it would be all smooth sailing After all, it was winter in Wisconsin, and this was a bad one. He also had heard in the forecast that there was some wind out there, maybe gusting, and gusting could mean treacherous driving, especially for an empty truck driving through the snow-covered flatlands of fallow fields as far as the eye could see, although Bill was perfectly aware that no one could see very far at this hour of the night.

At the moment, his truck was empty, lacking the weight that gave him greater stability on the road. He'd have to watch it until he got to Chicago. Even so, after loading up, he knew he'd be driving across a lot of flatland and that usually meant a lot of wind, even when it wasn't in the forecast. His starting point was Chicago, the Windy City, and thinking about that was enough to make him grip the steering wheel a fraction more firmly. Maybe his inner voice or a sixth sense spoke to him at that very moment because, just then, a gust of wind took a jab at his truck. It hit the side of his trailer with a solid blow, like a fighter working the bag with fresh arms. Bill took it. And he took another one moments later, just as hard as the first. It was the third jab a minute later that hurt the most, catching the tail end of the trailer and knocking the back right wheels slightly off the pavement onto the graveled and iced-over shoulder.

Bill overcompensated, steering his truck over the center line, fearful he wouldn't be able to jump the back wheels back onto the pavement. At the instant he crossed the center line, he thanked his lucky stars that there was no other traffic on the road, behind him or in front of him. The back wheels made the jump back on, but Bill had yet to regain control of his rig. Just as he turned slightly to bring it back into his lane, another beastly punch of wind scored big and pushed his whole trailer sideways, shoving the front and back axels of wheels a full three feet toward the edge of the pavement. His cab shook furiously against the counterweight of the trailer.

Bill was in dire straits now and literally didn't know which way to turn to get control back, when suddenly his truck ceased reacting to him at all, its tires spinning out in the unpaved shoulder, causing the side of the truck to slide into the compacted ten-foot snow wall that had been created by countless runs of snowplows that had cleared snowfall after snowfall from the highway over a period of many weeks. For a second, the truck looked like a big bobsled rounding a curve, its side pressed against the outside track wall by centrifugal force.

Then, suddenly, the cab lurched violently back onto the highway, the cab and trailer jackknifed, and the whole rig flipped onto its side, rolled over once, and skidded down the deserted highway in a trail of sparks for one hundred yards before coming to a grinding halt, at which point, it was straddling both lanes. Its driver was bounced around inside his cab like dice in a dice cup hoping for a seven or eleven on the first roll. He wasn't lucky. Bill Jankowicz, dead at age thirty-eight. Just like that, on the same highway Connie and Carl were traveling. He had crashed just a bit beyond their turnoff.

This horrendous rollover was over within a matter of seconds. Bill's fight to regain control of his truck had lasted less than twenty seconds. Five minutes earlier he had been as happy as a lark, singing "Sentimental Journey" with Doris Day, and then—pow!—his world was upended. It all had happened while he was heading southbound, only a mile south of Quinney, a couple of miles before Carl and Connie's turnoff to Chilton. They would never see Bill's truck as it lay across the highway. They would be turning off State Road 55 to go to Chilton two miles before the crash site. Someone else would discover the accident scene and Bill's lifeless body.

Life is generally unpredictable—we all know that—and, of course, so is Death's knock. And most of us know that our situation is the outcome of choices we make. What we don't know is how often Death moves around us—how close it comes at times, almost stalking us in silence, cloaked in invisibility, lurking, sometimes getting within a whisper of our ear, waiting perhaps for us to make a misstep into a point of no return or take a miscue or have a sudden lapse in attention to our life force. Death is out there, although no one wants to think about that, of course. But it is out there, and often it comes suddenly, unexpectedly, and so fast that we're in its deathly clutches before we know it. Bill Jankowicz is proof of that. But I digress.

CHAPTER FOURTEEN

Carl and Connie were making good time, a mile a minute, since getting on the highway. They were already twenty miles outside of Fond du Lac, which meant less than ten miles from Chilton. The surface of the road was dry, and there was almost no other traffic. Only a couple of cars passed them going the other way, toward Fond du Lac, and they hadn't seen any going in their direction. About two miles ahead, County Road 151 split off from State Road 55 to the right, which was their turnoff to Chilton. Connie sat up suddenly, aware of their proximity to the final leg to Chilton. She was anxious to get to Mama and Henry's, and she wanted nothing more than to go to sleep in Carl's arms as soon as possible and wake up to a big breakfast where she could announce her exciting news about the baby.

Carl and Connie briefly glanced at each other a mile before their turnoff, swapping a small smile that said a lot.

"Connie," Carl paused after saying her name, breaking into their shared silence, then searching a couple of seconds for the words he wanted, words that would probably not be ones Connie wanted to hear, "uh... I'm thinking we should just keep going, make it back to Appleton tonight." He made the statement, expressing his sudden desire in a change of plans, but he asked it a bit like a question and then waited for her reaction.

"What?" Connie said, clearly surprised and then looked at him. "I thought we'd agreed to spend the night at Mama and Henry's. Besides," she continued, "it's a lot closer than home, and... and they're expecting us." Connie's mind jumped to a vision of Sunday breakfast and her announcement and all the excitement that would follow with her news about the baby.

"I know they're expecting us, honey," he paused, "but we stayed with them just two weeks ago, and I've got some stuff I want to work on tomorrow at home, you know—maybe get into the office early and change a few drawings for the Conway's home in Menasha."

"Can't that wait?"

"Well... not really. I got some great ideas tonight talking to Bob Brumder—you know Bob, right?—and since I'm meeting with the Conways on Monday afternoon... well, I'd really like to have those ideas on paper for them."

"Oh Carl," Connie's voice was deflated and had slipped into pleading, "I want to be with Mama and Henry this weekend... puh-leeeeze."

"Baby, we spend a lot of time with them as it is. You know I love them." He waited a beat. "I have to do this work. Really. It's too important."

"Carl, please, Carl," she begged, feeling a desire to have her way that surprised her; its strength couldn't be explained. "Let's stay there tonight, and then we can leave right after breakfast." Now both her hands were clenching his right upper arm as she leaned into him and looked into his face as he focused on the road. "Carl," she implored him, "puh-leeeeeze, honey, pleeeeze. We can be home by noon. That'll give you all afternoon to work on your ideas."

The turnoff was two hundred yards up ahead and Carl

wasn't slowing down.

"Carl, please. Turn here. Please." Connie pleaded and pleaded, realizing just then that they were going too fast to make the turn.

"Sorry, Connie," Carl stated, clearly his mind had been made up. "There's just too much to do. Ruby and Henry will understand." Carl blew past the turnoff and continued up the highway. He felt Connie's disappointment as she slouched back into her seat. He tried to soothe her. "I'm sorry, baby. I just think we should get home tonight. You can call them first thing in the morning. Maybe next weekend we'll come down." The decision had been made. The turnoff had disappeared in the darkness behind them.

Connie didn't say anything; her disappointment overwhelmed her. "This is so unlike Carl," she thought to herself, and she resigned herself to postponing the announcement of her pregnancy, accepting his decision but not liking it. "He must have some big ideas he's anxious to put on paper," she told herself. With acceptance of Carl's decision to push on, she hugged herself with the consolation that she would be in his arms in their own bed in twenty-five minutes, and they would have a delicious morning waking up together, if she didn't have a bout of morning sickness, something Carl hadn't yet noticed. They didn't say another word to each other. Connie acquiesced, folded her hands over her tummy, thinking of the life growing inside of her, then closed her eyes and whispered, "I love you, Carl."

Carl kept the pace up, cruising steadily at five miles over the limit. He expected they'd be home in twenty minutes, especially with no traffic. They flew north, cutting through the dark night with only their headlights leading the way. A minute later, while he was taking a curve in the road, he glanced at his beautiful sleeping wife, and in the instant when his eyes returned to the road, he saw something big and dark, illuminated in his headlights, dead center in front of him, right in his path, just a few feet out there. He screamed because he suddenly knew what it was before he even had a chance to hit the brakes—but knowing didn't make a difference. Connie instinctively jumped to alertness, opened her eyes, roused from her stupor, and looked at Carl, all this in less than a second.

Nothing made a difference. It was too late; the collision was underway. She watched as Carl flew through the windshield in an explosion of broken glass, headfirst into the chassis of Bill Jankowicz's truck. Connie went with Carl, doing the same, together. It all happened so fast—and then, it was over. The cold darkness engulfed them, but winter's bone-chilling cold would never be as cold as death.

CHAPTER FIFTEEN

Vernon Koenig was driving north out of Fond du Lac on his way to Appleton in his 1941 Ford half-ton pickup truck. He was the first on the scene, maybe two minutes behind Connie and Carl. He, himself, had almost become a part of the carnage and would have, had it not been for the fact that he was driving his pickup truck extremely slowly, taking care not to scratch its expensive cargo, a top of the line casket tied down in the bed of his truck. He was a student at Lawrence University in Appleton, working his way through college by making deliveries with his truck. At least once a month, he'd haul a new casket or two between the two mortuaries owned by the Krause Funeral Homes, one in Fond du Lac and one in Appleton.

His headlights instantly revealed what had happened—something awful, beyond anything his imagination could come up with. Vernon stopped twenty feet short of the twisted, smoking mass of obliterated metal frames, doors and fenders, and everything else that makes up a truck and a car. He didn't know how it had happened, and he didn't need to. It was evident to him that there had been a very bad collision, most likely a head on, he was thinking, because what he saw was two vehicles that were entirely merged, but it was hard to tell in that grotesquely twisted mass of metal. He knew there would be bodies in the mess, although he couldn't see any from his

66

truck. He jumped out of his truck and walked slowly, fearful of what he might see and not believing anyone could possibly have survived an accident like that.

As he walked, he saw another set of headlights coming his way from the north and was immediately fearful that they hadn't yet seen the vehicles piled across the road. His fears quickly dissipated, as the oncoming vehicle slowed to a stop on the other side of the collision. He and the other people, a young couple named Alice and Eli, ran up to each other, all horrified by the scene in front of them, which was now illuminated on both sides by their headlights. Two more pairs of headlights were creeping up to the scene, and the danger of it getting worse seemed to be over.

Already shivering from the cold, the threesome immediately knew they needed to undertake the ghoulish task of finding the bodies, although Alice hung back, frozen more by fear of what they might find than by the rapidly descending temperature. Eli and Vernon spoke loudly to each other of their hope to find someone alive, but in their hearts, they couldn't imagine that anyone could possibly have survived the impact that had occurred, and each quickly concluded that no one could have survived in that cold for very long, in any condition, especially injured. God Almighty, it was cold. Nonetheless, the two men quickly moved in because they could see bodies, or what looked like bodies. Discovery took less than a minute.

Eli was the first to call out: "Truck driver's dead!" He saw that the driver was literally squished in the cab, which had collapsed like a crushed Dixie cup.

Vernon stopped a few feet short of the mangled steel of what was once the frontend of the car, looking as if it had tried to insert itself into the heavy steel underbelly of the truck. There wasn't much left of either vehicle that could be identified as front or back or any particular piece. Then he saw two mangled bodies, almost side by side, their torsos wrapped in bloody coats. Blood was everywhere around them.

Eli stepped up to Vernon's side, both less than five feet from the driver's body, or what must have been the driver. The body was headless, and the head had ceased to exist in any shape that was recognizable as a head. Brains, or what looked like brains, were mixed everywhere with viscera spewing out of the neck. It was a big red mess that turned their stomachs. Eli turned around, buckled over, and emptied the contents of his stomach on the pavement.

Vernon stepped forward. He had seen injured and dead bodies at the mortuaries, but that didn't make it easy to accept what was in front of him. Moving his eyes slowly in the poor lighting over the other body, he took yet another step closer. It could be a woman, he thought to himself. He could see long, blood-soaked, blonde hair and a hand grotesquely entwined in the strands. Suddenly, the hand twitched.

Vernon nearly jumped out of his boots. He leaned forward and held his breath, willing himself to have a steady eye and praying that he would see some more movement, that it wasn't just his imagination. The hand moved again, barely.

"Help!" he cried out. "Help! Someone's alive! She's alive!"

Ten minutes later, five men and two women had, by sheer strength and courage in the face of this nightmare, miraculously extricated Connie from the twisted cage of steel and glass. It wouldn't have been possible without some light from a couple of flashlights and muscle-straining work with a crowbar and a pike.

"God Almighty!" Eli called out upon seeing her set on the ground. He gagged again, but with his stomach already emptied, nothing came up this time.

Vernon cried out to Connie's mangled body at his feet, not believing it would do any good, but he couldn't help himself— he had to try: "You'll be all right, ma'am. You'll be all right!" He could barely recognize her battered body as a person. It was a miracle he could find his voice; no one else could find theirs. The sight of her was not for the faint-hearted. Those who had pulled her from the wreckage stood around the amorphous body that was covered in blood, not believing it held onto life—yet it did—and not believing that there was any hope, believing that death must be only minutes away for this poor soul, mercifully.

Connie lay on the cold, hard ground, unconscious on a blanket that someone had thrown down. Not much light was getting to her from the headlights of the surrounding cars, but flashlights were in a couple of hands. Strangers whom tragedy had brought together, numbering six or seven, saw something shockingly sorrowful as Connie lay there, her life force ebbing.

Eli had regained his composure. Although still dizzy, he saw that her jaw had been torn away and was hanging on the side of her head, attached only because a tendon on that side hadn't been severed. Alice saw an eyeball dangling down the other side of Connie's face, if "face" is what you could call what was there. Pieces of glass from the windshield that were embedded in her face eerily sparkled when caught in the light of their flashlights. For a second, it looked to Vernon like a leg was missing, but it was there, under her, folded under her and connected only by a sleeve of skin. Both of her arms were akimbo with splintered bones blatantly protruding.

Blood was everywhere, and it kept flowing. Warm and sticky, it got on everyone who had lent a hand. Less than a minute had passed since they had set her down, and they had to do something fast. Everyone knew that every second could mean the difference between life and death, although no one imagined that any one of the people standing over Connie had any hope. That this mangled woman could survive an accident like this could only mean a miracle. No one believed a miracle was in the making. No one.

Vernon was the first to break the silence of shock and cut through the miasma of death and despair. "Get her up," he yelled, "Lift her up in that blanket! Use it like a hammock. Get her up, I say—quickly!" He continued to yell, which was the only way he knew to conquer his fear. "I've got a casket in the bed of my truck. Let's put her in it!" He took command but was still yelling, and it was all he could do to stop his shivering. Everyone else was shivering too. "C'mon, move, people! I'll open the casket! You put her in, close it, and I'll drive like hell to St. Agnes in Fond du Lac!" He ran to his truck twenty-five feet away, jumped up on the bed, and with his pocketknife, cut the rope around the protective canvas so that he could get to the casket and open it up. His hands were too cold to untie the knots.

Some other man, a latecomer to the scene, took charge of the group in an effort to carry Connie in the blanket up to the open casket. No one believed they could save her, but no one wanted to believe they couldn't. Once she was in it, it registered with Vernon that she was bleeding all over the satin bed and side panels. He'd have to deal with Mr. Krause later. Vernon slammed the coffin lid down. He wasn't worried about her not getting any air; he was more worried about the deathly frigid air getting her. He prayed that she wouldn't bleed out.

Vernon wasted no time. Upon making a u-turn and getting clear of the other cars, he put his foot to the gas pedal, and the Ford pickup's V-8 lurched forward, as Vernon took it through all three gears as quickly as possible. Just a short time ago he was taking his time driving up to Appleton, and now he was about to drive like a bat out of hell back to Fond du Lac to get this dying woman to the hospital, maybe—maybe—in time to save her life. He left the scene, and everyone ran to their cars for heat. Most would wait for the police to show up, while providing a warning to other drivers so that no one else would get killed. There was safety in numbers. They could wait— Connie couldn't.

Truly, every fork in our lives has meaning, and every choice puts us down a different path. We will never know where we would have gone had we taken another route, nor could we guess the outcome of the choices we didn't make. Never. By the time we understand something about the one we did take, well, we're probably facing another fork, and another, and another after that. As we move through life, as a result of these forks and the choices we make, we all become self-made—but only the millionaires admit it. But I digress.

CHAPTER SIXTEEN

Vernon drove his truck faster than he had ever driven in his life. He had no idea what the highest speed was that his truck could attain, until that night. Within three blocks of the hospital, a police car picked him up, turned on its flashing lights and siren, and ran up his tailpipe, undoubtedly thinking he was about to write a ticket for a speeding violation. Vernon didn't slow down. Once there, at St. Agnes, he drove up the emergency drive and slammed on his brakes six feet from the entrance. The cop's flashing lights got everyone's attention, but nothing made them jump like the image of a blood-spattered, crazed young man bursting through the doors, screaming for help.

At first, the duty nurse thought Vernon was a victim of a mugging because he was covered head to toe in blood. The policeman burst through the doors behind him, suggesting he had made an accurate assessment of Vernon's situation. Three emergency room assistants appeared from different rooms, responding to the sudden chaos of Vernon's intrusion. The duty nurse, thirty-four year old Helen Kaplan, already a veteran in emergency trauma, remained calm and coolly picked up her phone and dialed the office of Dr. Ernst von Hoerner, the physician who was on duty for the night.

Vernon frantically explained himself and described the accident scene in a matter of precious seconds and then directed all hands to his truck and, specifically, to the bed of the truck, where the coffin was, which had been strapped to the floor of the bed. Vernon led the way, leaping onto the bed of the truck in a single bound, fueled by a high level of adrenaline. He yanked open the heavy coffin lid as two assistants stood alongside him on the flatbed with baited breath over the expectation that Vernon had created.

They gasped at the sight—a horribly mutilated, bloody human being of such gruesome proportions that they winced visibly despite their many years of experience handling emergencies. One of the ER assistants moved in on the body, searching for vital signs, although the leakage of blood from a couple of gaping wounds suggested this person, apparently a woman, was still alive. The ER person confirmed his finding, "She's alive!" With that, the two ER assistants grabbed the hammocked blanket and lifted Connie out of the casket and into the waiting arms of others, who placed her on a gurney and ran with it into the hospital.

Connie moved within herself, within the deepness of herself, feeling lost and disconnected and in an existence that floated in and out of spaces she did not know, moving in an ether of nothingness, somewhere in an unknown space. She felt nothing—no pain, no cold, no warmth—just a kind of stillness when she was wheeled into the hospital on that gurney, blasted suddenly by bright lights. Images came and went, most making little or no sense, although she momentarily saw Carl, or some vaporous image of Carl that swirled into the nothingness like a dust devil. Then she saw her face in a mirror, the same image she had seen when Carl and she were leaving their apartment, but this time, there was no mirror, only an image of her face, floating as if it were a reflection in a pool of water. The face—

her face—spoke to her again. This time it only whispered the words "You will never see me again," then the image faded, and Connie fell into a crevasse of unconsciousness.

Vernon had stepped back toward the cab of his truck and leaned back on it moments after the two ER men had joined him on the bed of the truck. He collapsed, exhausted, and debilitated by the experience, immersed in the steam of his overheated body and unable to move, numb to what he would do next. The cop jumped up and helped him down to the ground and then escorted him into the hospital, where Vernon would be safe from the biting cold and, if necessary, could get some medical attention.

As it turned out, moments after entering the waiting area, Vernon collapsed again, this time in the police officer's arms, from total exhaustion and shock, but not in a medical sense. He was simply traumatized by the events of the night. He was checked into St. Agnes for the night for observation. Moments after he had been helped into one of the hospital beds, he felt the downward pull of the sedative that he'd been given. Just before it kicked in, he said a prayer for that poor woman and hoped that he had saved her life, although maybe, he thought to himself, it would be a blessing if she went to a better place. Who, he wondered, could possibly recover from those injuries? Surely they would tell him in the morning if the woman had made it or not. His eyes closed with heavy, heavy lids, and he slipped into the nothingness of a deep sleep, coerced by sedatives.

Connie was already on the operating table, and Dr. von Hoerner was scrubbing up, when the duty nurse, Lucinda Barnes, solved the mystery of the injured woman's identity. She burst into the prep room to share her discovery with the doctor.

"Dr. von Hoerner," she blurted out, "the victim didn't have a purse with her, but I found a letter in her coat pocket that was addressed to Mrs. Carl Koehler, and the letter begins 'Dear Connie.'" Nurse Barnes looked at the doctor, wanting to know if he recognized the name. She thought that he might because Dr. von Hoerner, who had been serving the community for fifty miles in every direction for over thirty years, knew almost everyone.

In the instant upon receiving the news, he gasped and looked upward, saying, "Oh my God, it's Connie Ortlieb! Call Ruby and Henry right away!"

"Ruby and Henry?" Nurse Barnes froze, seeking enlightenment.

"Yes, yes!" he exclaimed, "Ruby and Henry Steenport in Chilton. Call them right away! Waste no time! And Mrs. Von Hoerner… call her too, and tell her everything you can." Nurse Barnes paused momentarily, in case he wanted to add anything further. One of the attendants slipped on his surgical gloves as the doctor turned to her and said, "Go! Go! Go!"

Nurse Barnes was out of the prep room before the third "Go!" left Dr. von Hoerner's lips. He finished prepping, horrified that this trauma patient was Connie, the Connie he had delivered into this world twenty-five years ago.

Moments later, the doctor marched into the operating room, knowing that every second counted and the right decisions had to be made if there was to be any chance of survival. As he entered, he looked directly into the eyes of his senior operating assistant, Ida Voss, RN, a woman he had worked with for nearly as long as he had been practicing medicine, and through his surgical mask he said, "Ida, it's Connie Ortlieb," and then corrected himself, "Connie Koehler."

Connie heard her name spoken and then blacked out again.

"Connie! Oh Lord!" whispered Ida, "Oh my!" her voice rose, "Surely that means one of the accident victims was Carl! How horrible, horrible, just...," now exclaiming loudly, "HORRIBLE!" She looked up, momentarily stunned by the indiscretion of her raised voice. She strengthened her resolve, determined to do everything in her power to save Connie's life. She glanced downward at a woman clinging to life, a woman she had known her whole life time, and then looked up from Connie's mangled body, meeting Dr. von Hoerner's experienced gaze and calmly said, "Let's hope we can save her."

"Yes, of course," he replied. "Now let's get to work!" Six people moved around the room, each with specific tasks, all doubtful that this life could be saved, but all committed to doing everything they could. In a flurry of movement, Dr. von Hoerner leaned over Connie, who in her dire condition and arrival in an unconscious state, had just been anesthetized. He spoke directly to her, "Connie, this is Dr. von Hoerner. You will make it through this; just hang on." Everyone was moved by the doctor's words.

The surgery began, although it wasn't easy to know where to start—so many life threatening traumas were in play. The massive loss of blood concerned him the most, so first of all, he had to stop any further loss. He looked up at Ida and saw two wet spots on her surgical mask, just below her eyes, surely created by tears running down her cheeks. He would have to hold his own tears back; they could and would come later. He had known Ruby and Henry for the thirty years that he had been practicing medicine in Fond du Lac. He thought of them as the best people on earth. The tears would come, but right now he didn't have time to think about the heartbreak that was about to befall them.

No parent ever imagines that they will outlive their children. It is every parent's nightmare. The pain of losing a child is so great that those who have experienced this will tell you that this unspeakable heartbreak is a burden few can take and one that no one can overcome. All anyone can hope for is the strength to embrace life for all its mystery and move forward, despite its wicked cruelties, its Sisyphean burdens, and the heartless hands it can deal us. God works his miracles in many ways beyond our understanding. We just have to hang onto our love for life, which is a love for others, so that we may be part of those miracles. But I digress.

CHAPTER SEVENTEEN

At three in the morning, approximately two hours after the accident, Ruby and Henry walked into St. Agnes's emergency entrance. Nurse Kaplan was expecting them. She was the one who had called them—a call that was as difficult as any to make in her career. It was a call that she had made less than an hour ago.

When she called, Henry got out of bed, groggy from being rousted out of a good night of sleep by the intrusive and incessant ring of the phone. His step was a bit unsteady, and his legs a bit stiff when he walked into the kitchen to answer it. Ruby sat up in bed, knowing that no phone call at that hour was one that carried good news. Instantly, she was worried sick with a mother's instinct. She held her breath, listening acutely and wanting Henry to return to the room and say, "It's nothing, Ruby, a wrong number. Go back to sleep." She could hear his voice but couldn't understand what he was saying except for the words that caused her to climb out of bed and run to the kitchen when Henry cried out, "Oh God, no!... not Connie!"

Ruby ran to Henry's side and grabbed the old phone so that they could both listen to the voice on the other end of the line.

"I'm afraid so, Mr. Steenport. Dr. von Hoerner insisted that I call you right away and tell you to come to St. Agnes's emergency desk."

"You say she's alive?" Henry asked, his voice already

choking up.

"Yes, yes!" the voice on the other end of the line said, "She's alive, but it's not good." Upon hearing those words, Ruby screamed and slumped to the floor and wrapped her arms around Henry's legs, already heaving in tears, thinking about what it all must mean. "You must hurry, Mr. Steenport. Dr. von Hoerner is already in surgery."

Henry wanted to know more. "What about Carl, her husband? The man in the car with her... what happened to him?"

"Oh, Mr. Steenport, I don't know if I can tell you that. I can't be sure. I only heard things."

"Dammit, woman!" Henry swore, half in anger and half in deep anguish."

"I'm sorry," the voice said with great sorrow.

"Tell me!" Henry implored. "What do you know? Please tell me."

The pain of this conversation was taking its toll on Nurse Kaplan. It was so difficult, and she felt so badly to be the bearer of this heartrending news. She raised herself up in her seat, seeking the inner strength to share what little she knew. "I heard there were two other people in the accident, two men. Mr. Steenport, I am so, so sorry, but I've been told they are both dead."

Henry knew one of those men was Carl—it had to be. He took a deep breath. "My wife and I will be there as soon as we can—within the hour." He hung up, drained already, and feeling a bottomless emptiness in his heart that he knew would never be filled. He knew he had to be strong; it was the only way that Ruby and he would get through this, and he was sure the worst was yet to come.

Henry lifted his tearful wife to her feet and hugged her and hugged her and hugged her, swaying with her in a veil of shared tears.

After a couple of minutes of sobbing, Ruby, enveloped in his arms, looked up into Henry's face and asked a question she didn't want to ask, "What about Carl?"

Henry looked up at the ceiling, wondering how he could possibly find the strength to say anything, but he had to; Ruby had to know. He gently tilted Ruby's head onto his chest so that it was secure under his chin and placed his open hand to the back of her head, like one might hold an infant, while his other was around her back, supporting her. He took a deep breath, tightly closing his eyes, not wanting to believe what he was about to say. "Ruby, Carl's dead."

Ruby's heart could have stopped right there; the pain was so great. She screamed in anguish again and heaved heavy tears as she clutched at Henry, as Henry pulled her tightly into his arms. Finally, she stopped; they both knew that they had to get to the hospital—they had to be with Connie. She pulled back a few inches from Henry, her face soaked with tears. "Henry," she could barely get the words out, "we have to be strong for Connie." He nodded, looking at her with his own tears streaming down his face. "Let's get dressed and go to the hospital right away. C'mon, we should go now." They pulled apart and did what they had to do to get to the hospital in what would easily be the most sorrow-filled drive of their lives.

There is probably no limit to the compassion we human beings can feel for our fellow human beings. We hurt so much at times, in every way, when we see that others are hurting. It is a bonding agent, common to all humans, regardless of where they live, regardless of their culture, regardless of their beliefs.

Compassion is one of those things that makes us distinctly human—we feel for each other, for all human beings: another person's suffering is our suffering. Sometimes life can be so brutal and, sadly, sharing the experience is sometimes all we have to keep us going. But I digress.

CHAPTER EIGHTEEN

Ruby and Henry had been waiting on a wooden bench in the hallway between emergency admittance and the main hospital rooms for hours, with a view of the main door into the hospital's section of operating rooms. A horrible, horrible night was coming to a close, but the nightmare continued and would for a long time. How long? Years? Maybe years. Maybe a lifetime. The frosted window panes that were arranged in a geometry of small glass blocks at the top of the wall opposite from them went indiscernibly from black to gray to white as the sun rose on another desperately cold winter day.

Both were exhausted, crestfallen, and wrung out like an old dish rag after its last tub of pots and pans at a cheap diner. Sleep provided snatches of mercy while they waited patiently and forlorn on the hard seat of the bench for word from Dr. von Hoerner. Henry looked at his watch and estimated that von Hoerner was finishing up his sixth straight hour in the operating room, working on Connie every minute. The agony of waiting took its toll, but both Ruby and Henry knew that Connie was still alive as long as the doctor was still in the operating room. They waited patiently—there was nothing else they could do, nothing else but pray, and pray they did, for hours.

Ten minutes into the growing light of another cold day, Ruby and Henry's neighbors, Ike and Isabel Luick, walked through the hospital's doors and spotted Ruby and Henry sitting alone on a bench, their sorrowful state of despair accentuated by the long, starkly lit, sterile hall of the hospital, which was cut up by the harsh shadows from ceiling lights that were as big as street lamps, setting up a contrast between the hardness of the hospital's interior and the softness of the these two souls. They hurried over to the exhausted, rumpled couple they had known all their lives. Chilton was a small town, and just about everyone knew everyone else, and just about every adult who had grown up there was a friend of everyone else who had grown up there.

Henry looked up, having sensed movement. He rose to shake hands with Ike, extending his hand out, but instead Ike embraced him, and the two old friends just bear-hugged. Henry let a tear escape onto Ike's shoulder. Isabel moved in to be at Ruby's side, placing her arm around her and hugging her in the silence of so much grief. No one talked; the pain overwhelmed all four of them, as the foursome sat and shared the long bench. A minute later, Robert Uihlein entered the hospital and approached the foursome. He, too, was an old friend.

"Hank," Robert whispered his name. Henry stood up again, drained as he was, and the two old friends embraced. Robert wouldn't let go; he wanted so badly to absorb his friend's sorrow into his own being and to do whatever he could to lighten Henry's heavy heart. He was the only one of Henry's friends who called him Hank. They had known each other since they were teenagers and said each other's name whenever someone wanted to know who their best friend was.

After awhile, the two men broke apart, and with Robert's motion to him to sit down, he seated himself once again on the bench, next to his Ruby, his head dropped into his hands, bending over to set his elbows onto his knees. Isabel sat on the other side of Ruby, her arms around her fully and gently rocked and cooed softly into Ruby's ear when she wasn't saying, "Connie will make it through this, Ruby, don't worry. She's strong, and she'll make it through this," adding, "and you and Henry will too. God will give you the strength." Robert remained standing, absorbing more sorrow than he feared he could handle.

Robert and Ike looked at each other in their shared commiseration over the tragedy. "Did the doc's wife call you too?" Robert asked.

"Ya," Ike stood up and replied. Then he tilted his head, indicating that the two of them should walk down the hall a bit. After ten paces of silence, Ike spoke softly saying, "I think the whole town must know by now." Several seconds of silence passed before he continued. "Marge called just before dawn—woke us up. I told Isabel and looked out the window and saw lights on in Henry's house and went over there. They had already left... I thought I heard a car pull out in the middle of the night... but I didn't think nothin' of it, ya know. Nothing much ever happens in Chilton... I mean nothin' like crime or this, ya know."

"What about Carl's family?" Robert asked.

"Jumpin' Jesus, I'd hate to be the one that delivered that news." He shook his head. "Such an awful thing. Carl... dead! *Gott in Himmel!*" he swore, slipping momentarily into the language of his German immigrant parents. He let out a lungful of air through tight lips and continued, "After Marge called me, I think she was going to look into it, ya know, call the highway police and see what they were doing."

"I bet Carl's folks already know," Robert said. "How could

they survive hearing that Carl's dead? Holy Christmas!"

"I think the doc's wife called Carl's family. Oh ya, I do, Robert. Marge has made those calls before."

"I hope I never get another call from her in the middle of the night. It's no good when the phone rings in the middle of the night and it's the doc's wife."

"Nope," Ike agreed, "never is."

"You think Carl's parents are on their way here?"

"Oh gosh, I don't see how. They must be... I dunno... I don't think so. Not now. Maybe later," Ike sighed.

Robert cut in, "You mean if there is a later."

"Don't talk like that, Robert! Of course there will be a later. Don't think there's any other outcome than Connie bein' all right. Now dontcha, Robert, dontcha be sayin' nothin' like that!"

"God dammit!" Robert said in a sudden tone of anger, driven as much by fear as anything. "I'm sorry, Ike. Of course she'll make."

The two men got to the end of the hall, turned, and at that moment, saw Dr. von Hoerner walk into the hallway, approaching the bench where Ruby and Henry sat. He wasn't wearing his surgical scrubs. Henry jumped to his feet. Ruby and Isabel stood up with him and moved forward to greet him, to get his news, their eyes beading on him, with deeply hopeful expressions on their faces. Ike and Robert picked up their pace and moved quickly up the hall to them, missing the first few words on Connie's status. They could tell from the reactions that she hadn't died. No one was convulsive, although no one was smiling, of course.

"God and Jesus Almighty," said Robert, turning briefly to Ike, "pray that the news is good!" Ike didn't have time to respond before the two men joined the foursome. It was time to listen to what Dr. von Hoerner was saying. They stepped in with the doctor's prognosis underway.

"… a long time before we can be sure about anything," said von Hoerner. She's stabilized, if I can say that, but the accident was so traumatic that… well, I have to tell you, there's a lot more surgery ahead of her, maybe—I'm sorry—maybe for years. As it is, it's a miracle that she's still with us."

"Thank the Lord," exclaimed Ruby, biting hard on her lower lip.

Von Hoerner continued with his prognosis, "Let's just pray that she pulls out of this first round of surgeries well enough to get to the next round. Her injuries are extensive. In six hours, we did a lot… had to… so many injuries. Yep, it's a miracle, I have to say. I can tell you that much." He paused, but no one said anything, so he continued. He tried to sound more upbeat. "Connie is a tough cookie. Every time I ever saw her for something, she always bounced back. That's a good thing for someone up against what she is." He paused again. There were still no interruptions—everybody was hanging on his every word. "I say she's stabilized, but there's been a lot of blood loss. We don't know yet what the outcome of that will be." That's when Henry interrupted.

"Whatdya mean, Doc? What do you mean, 'the outcome'? She's going to get out of all this just fine, eventually… right?"

Remember, dear reader, Ruby and Henry and their friends weren't at the accident and they weren't in the emergency room when Connie arrived in a coffin in Vernon Koenig's flat bed pickup truck over six hours ago. Actually, it was probably a good thing that they didn't know everything; knowing would have sucked every ounce of hope out of them.

Dr. von Hoerner searched for the right words to answer Henry's question. At a time like that, the right words were very important—he knew that—but he didn't want to give anyone false hope. "Hard to say, Henry. We're in pretty tricky territory here. By the time she arrived, she'd lost so much blood... well... there may be some permanent damage. Traumatic head injuries have outcomes that are difficult to predict. That's down the pike. Too many other things need attention now. She's clearly not out of the woods and may not be for quite some time. Besides the massive head trauma, just about every bone was fractured... not her spine, though... another miracle... and...," he paused again, "she lost her left eye for sure." Then he quickly added, "The other one's okay," not wanting them to worry that she had lost her sight entirely.

"God Almighty in heaven," Henry muttered, his heart convulsed with the news. He hugged Ruby, drawing her into him, afraid she'd collapse from hearing what the doctor had just said.

Dr. von Hoerner stood in a moment of silence, looking at Ruby first, then Henry. "I don't know if I can save her right leg. It's pretty bad." He knew that was a huge understatement. "We've got it intact at the moment," he reassured everyone, "but I'll have to return to surgery in a few minutes and decide... well, I'll have to decide what to do with that leg. I can't say for sure if I can save it."

Henry cut in quickly. "Doc, you gotta save her leg." Henry got emotional, although his emotions must have surely been spent. "Don't cut her leg off, Doc. Don't do it...." And then Henry surprised everyone by saying, "You cut it off—it'll be over my dead body." That was his way of making his point.

Dr. von Hoerner looked at him earnestly and understood.

He had seen great love expressed in strong words like that before, and then he looked at Ruby, so pale and worn. All she could do was look up at him and barely nod her head. He understood everything in her nod: how she felt and what she hoped for, willing him to do his best with all of the energy she had left, which clearly wasn't much. He turned back to face Henry. "Henry," he said, "I'll do everything in my power, but I can't promise you anything."

It hurt him to deliver such news, news that would strain any parent's heart and push them into realms of disbelief and shock. After a sigh, Dr. von Hoerner said, "There's more bad news I have to tell you." Henry froze, waiting for what he expected would be another punch to the gut. He wasn't sure he could take another one. Ruby, her head down, eyes closed, looked up ready to take yet another rip in her heart.

"What is it, Doc?" Henry asked, breaking the prelude of silence.

Dr. von Hoerner glanced at Henry, then taking Ruby's hands, he led her to the bench and motioned with his head for her to sit down. Isabel sat on one side of her, and Henry took his place on the other side. Ike and Henry remained standing, flanking Dr. von Hoerner. They all looked at him, frozen in pain, awaiting the delivery of more bad news.

In the softest voice yet, Dr. von Hoerner said directly to Ruby, "She lost the baby."

Ruby and Henry's eyes welled up and released tears that they had been holding back. Ruby covered her face and bent over sobbing. Henry put his arm around her, shocked, but found his voice, "Doc, we didn't know she was pregnant."

"Oh, God Almighty," said Dr. von Hoerner, "I am so sorry I am the bearer of all this horrible, horrible news." He paused again, debating whether or not he should share more bad news. But, however painful, they had a right to know. "Her pelvis is broken in six places. It's very complicated, it might heal, but I doubt she'll ever be able to have children." Once again, he said, "I'm so sorry." No one moved, and there was no sound except for Ruby's sobbing.

"I've got to get back in there," he said. "There's more surgery to be done before I can leave," he spoke calmly, having regained his professional composure. "Dr. Drake will be joining me and then staying after me for some follow up. She'll be in the operating room for several more hours. I've done everything I can so far… a bit more for me to do, but like I said, Dr. Drake will take over. I'll be back here in a couple of hours." With that, Dr. von Hoerner said, "Don't give up. She'll make it through all this, yes, she will." He turned and walked through the doors that led back to the operating rooms, out of the sight of five very distraught people, five people who loved Connie very much and felt such great sorrow for the Koehlers.

Henry stayed seated, now turned inward toward Ruby with both arms around her, his head against hers. "We'll stay right here—wait for the doc to come back." Neither of them could imagine any other option. They wanted to be there for Connie when she came to, and they knew that was a ways off.

Ike was the first to speak. "I'll go out and get some coffee and some food for all of us." Robert looked at him and said, "No, Ike, you stay here with Isabel, and the two of you wait with Hank and Ruby. I'll go."

"Thanks Robert," Ike responded and looked at Isabel, "We'll stay with them."

"Back in thirty minutes," Robert said and then walked down the hallway, through the entrance area of the emergency room, and out the door.

Five minutes later, Dr. von Hoerner was back at the operating table, this time with Dr. Drake at his side. They were surrounded by the emergency team staff, the same individuals that had been with von Hoerner from the start, all united in their mission to save Connie's life, all anxiously awaiting the appearance of another surgical team, since their energy was almost tapped out. Dr. von Hoerner was nearly spent and, truly, gave it his best. Now he was focused on saving Connie's leg with a little bit of renewed impetus from Henry. The immediate life and death needs had been met. He was thinking Connie just might make it through this horrendous calamity, but it was too early to hope for too much. Connie had a long way to go; he just didn't know exactly how long.

Every place we live has good things about it and not so good things. Most Americans in 1946 were living in small towns, from sea to shining sea, with a lot of farmland in between. America was still defined by its rural life and its small towns like Chilton, Wisconsin. Like it or not, in small town America, everyone knows what everyone else is doing, good or bad, from births and deaths to the kind of underwear a person wears, the latter thanks to backyard summer wash lines. In small towns, news spreads like a wild fire on a dry prairie blown over by warm winds. You learn to live with it, and when it works for you, you can be thankful because you discover how many people really care about you. And you know what? That number is often a lot bigger than what most people think. But I digress.

CHAPTER NINETEEN

Two hours later, Dr. von Hoerner entered the hallway outside the operating rooms once again, wanting to see Ruby and Henry, who were waiting and praying—mostly praying. They knew Connie was not out of the woods yet. As with anyone unfortunate enough to have to wait helplessly in the sterile environment of a hospital while a loved one is being operated on and hanging onto life by a thread, the ordeal was both mind-numbing and heartbreaking. In these instances, the worry and concern can be so great that no other thoughts are able to penetrate the dark and all-consuming mesh of fear and sorrow-filled soulful awareness of the misfortune. The thought that a positive outcome cannot be guaranteed pounces on one with the power of a raging grizzly in defense of her cubs.

Sleep can provide some relief, a respite, escape perhaps, but it is often so fitful that it may magnify the discomfort rather than providing solace. Sleep deprivation is a means of torture, and Ruby and Henry and their loyal friends could attest to the suffering they were experiencing as they waited for Connie's life to be secured. It was a suffering that was layered with the suffering that they knew Connie would experience once she was out of surgery and into a new world, a world that would present her with such overwhelming sadness that she might regret her life.

Dr. von Hoerner spied Ruby and Henry and their three

friends on the bench, seated side by side, silent and resting, exactly where he had left them a couple of hours ago. With their sudden awareness of his arrival, he put his palms up, suggesting that they stay seated. All obliged, almost delirious with the exhaustion caused by the worry that sapped them of their strength and spirit, yet all looked up hopefully, searching the doctor's face for a sign that the news would be good. He gave them that right away.

"We think Connie is going to be all right," von Hoerner said, opening with a tone of optimism, despite his evident fatigue. "As I said, she continues to respond. Stable, she is. The worst is behind her as far as the worst injuries."

Henry interrupted, "Can we see her, Doc?"

"Oh no. Not now, not for several hours. Too much to do still. Even with the critical injuries behind her, there's still several hours, at least," von Hoerner replied. "She'll be in post op care sometime later today, maybe late afternoon," he sighed, unsure of what he would say, and then continued, "for, well, quite some time, and she'll be heavily sedated till tomorrow anyway." He looked at them and read their expressions: all of them were wanting to know what they should do next. He had seen that look countless times in his vast experience.

Ruby and Henry didn't move; they just looked imploringly into Dr. von Hoerner's eyes, waiting for his next words.

"Now," von Hoerner said, "I think you all oughta go home, get some rest, collect yourselves. Come back tomorrow morning. That's what I'd do. Maybe call Carl's family." He looked at the floor, shaking his head and beginning to feel the exhaustion setting in, before continuing, "Sorry for the Koehlers too, so sorry."

He rose to his full height and then looked at everyone with

the confidence that gives birth to hope returning to his voice. "We've still got Connie with us, but there's nothing any of you can do here, at least not now. She'll be heavily sedated for a long time, maybe even a couple of days before we let her come to. I'll call you later today when I know more. Now go." His final two words, stated with such finality, was a command that had to be obeyed. They all stood up, and the five of them, united in grief, slowly walked out the emergency entrance and into air that was so cold and brutal that a breath of it stung their lungs, reminding them of how harsh life can be—not that they needed reminding.

How could each of them not ask themselves how Connie could possibly deal with her life now, which had been so upended as to be nearly unimaginable. Carl was gone, and with his eternal absence, there would be only memories of the perfect union he and Connie had had, only memories of times with Carl and Connie, only memories of the light they brought with them whenever they entered a room, only memories of the beautiful harmony of their spontaneously shared laughter. And now, the end of all their shared dreams was known. And who could not feel the loss of that special couple without feeling another arrow to the heart upon learning of the loss of the promise of a life that their unborn baby held? How infinite and immeasurable that joy would have been, and what joy would have been shared by anyone in contact with them. Who could not feel that loss and have the strength and daring to search for the right words to express it?

There would be no words, as no one would want the pain that would be invoked by saying anything more than that Carl was gone, Connie lost the baby, and her life would never, never be the same. Surely, she would not even appear to be the same person because of the scars. But a deeper humanity knows that the scars in the depths of her being would be the greatest, and they would never go away. At best, they could be lived with, but at that particular moment, no one would have thought that possible. Not even Connie.

Life is nothing without hope. No force is stronger than the life force within us. Evolution has assured us of that. Those born with the double helix that lacks "the will to live" gene don't get to pass their genes on and on through the march of time. Hope is what motivates the human spirit to go beyond its own limits, to do what some think cannot be done, to survive what people call the unsurvivable. Sometimes hope appears within us as a raging forest fire, inextinguishable and scorching in its passion, commanding us to live. And sometimes it is the smallest of flames, like a flicker of a candle that is so distant that we are beyond its heat. But I digress.

CHAPTER TWENTY

Dr. von Hoerner called Ruby and Henry later that afternoon, as he had promised, after everything that could be done for Connie had been done. He thought it best that they come in the next morning; they needed their rest after a grueling night waiting and then many hours of more waiting in the hallway that same morning. He reminded them that Connie was stabilized, informing them in the same breath that she was heavily sedated and surely experiencing no pain. Ruby and Henry decided after his call that they would get some rest, knowing they, indeed, needed it and nothing more could be done that day. They took Dr. von Hoerner's advice and said they'd come by in the morning around ten o'clock to look in on her.

Surprisingly, they both fell into a deep sleep that night rather than the expected fitful one. Refreshed on the heels of such a nourishing and badly needed night of sleep, they rose just before dawn. The ordeal had taken its toll, and they had no idea how exhausted they were with all that stress and worry. Both put their heads on the pillow that night at the same time, closed their eyes, and slept like the dead through the dead of night.

Ruby and Henry assembled themselves that morning and found themselves taking turns with nonstop phone calls from neighbors, friends, and anyone who knew them, all offering their sympathy and prayers and wanting to know how Connie was doing. It seemed the word was out about Carl's death. No one could really talk about that loss, other than a brief expression of sorrow, so shocking was that reality.

Ruby and Henry also made a call to Carl's parents, a most difficult and heartrending call, which they feared would make them speechless while drowning in their own tears. Their exchange over the phone was brief—about as long as it takes for a dagger plunged into the chest to penetrate the heart. Funeral arrangements would have to be made. The Koehler's would take care of that necessary business, a task that would challenge any adult's composure. No one expected Connie to take visitors for quite some time, although Ruby and Henry would be at her side within hours after rising.

It was only nine o'clock when Ruby and Henry walked into Connie's hospital room. She was completely covered in bandages, set into a body cast that cradled her entire frame from head to toe. The only skin that was exposed was some on her lower hands and wrists and her right eye. Tubes of all kinds took up the space on the wrists, and there were plenty of other tubes and wires coming out of different places in the body cast. The moment they saw her, Henry went speechless, while tears ran down Ruby's cheeks.

Dr. von Hoerner was expecting Connie to come to sometime early that morning, the best indicator being the opening of Connie's one good eye. As of that moment, her right eye hadn't opened, but that wasn't a surprise given what she had been through and the massive amount of sedatives in her system. Even so, this delayed response concerned Dr. von Hoerner, although he didn't say anything to Ruby and Henry at the time. He knew Connie's head injuries were extensive, and whether or not she had made it through the surgery couldn't be determined with any certainty quite yet. He made a mental note to have the nurse check on her frequently, seeking the critical moment when Connie opened that one good eye.

Ruby and Henry slowly approached Connie's bedside, not wanting to cause a disturbance of any kind. Touching the exposed flesh of Connie's hand was irresistible. It was the only link they could have with their traumatized daughter. Dr. von Hoerner pulled up the room's only two chairs and told them they could sit with her as long as they wanted. They both sat down with their chairs against the metal frame of the bed's side. Ruby held onto Connie's hand with one hand, and Henry held onto Ruby's other hand. Dr. von Hoerner and the attending nurse left the room, leaving Ruby and Henry alone with Connie.

Nearly eight hours later, at supper time, Ruby and Henry left and drove home, crestfallen. They would come back tomorrow and the next day and the next and would keep coming back to be with Connie to help her through what would obviously be a very long recovery.

Early the next morning, before Ruby and Henry arrived in Connie's room, Dr. von Hoerner was standing at Connie's bedside for the umpteenth time. She was breathing on her own. He noted on her chart that her vital signs were stable. She had made it through the first twenty-four hours of post op, except for one thing: she hadn't regained consciousness. Dr. von Hoerner shook his head, turned, and walked out of the room, as quietly as a human tear runs down a person's cheek, thinking she would have to stay in intensive care. Connie was in a coma.

The word coma comes from the Greek word *koma,* which means "deep sleep," but no one should ever think they are the same thing. Being in a coma has essentially nothing to do with sleep. Someone who is in a coma is unconscious and won't respond to voices or other sounds or to any activity nearby. This unconscious state may be prolonged and of an indeterminate length of time—possibly years, or in some unfortunate victims' life, possibly forever. Fortunately, most people come out of a coma.

The comatose person is still alive, of course, but the brain is functioning at only the lowest level of alertness. You can't shake or call out to a person in a coma with the hope of waking them up. Like I said, the person isn't asleep. Where are they? Nobody can really answer that question. It's likely that they don't know where they are either. We know that human beings often don't want to know the ugly truth. A coma is, perhaps, a survival mechanism. Maybe it is a way the subconscious protects itself from something that it might not have the strength to face. Of course, no one knows for sure. But I digress.

CHAPTER TWENTY-ONE

The car accident happened eight days ago. Ruby and Henry were making their eighth visit to Connie's room at St. Agnes Hospital. From their first visit, their routine was the same: they pulled the room's two chairs up to the bedside and talked to Connie. Dr. von Hoerner thought this was a good idea, even though Connie didn't respond to them—she couldn't—she was in a coma and had been lost in that deep crevasse since the accident. Even if she hadn't been in a coma, she wouldn't have been able to talk because her jaw had been wired shut, having been broken so severely. That it would have to be wired shut for the next two months was evidence of how severe the damage was to her lower face. As for the rest of her, she was in a full body plaster cast, with too many tubes running in and out for the layman to understand.

Ruby and Henry's two-hour visit that day differed from the previous visits in one respect: it was the first time someone else other than themselves and hospital staff was allowed to enter the room, and someone other than Father O'Reilly from St. Mary's, who was there on the third day after the accident to give her the Last Rights, just in case. This time, for the first time, they invited an old family friend, a man they had been close to for nearly fifty years, someone who Ruby shared her childhood with in Chilton. His name was Father Oliver. He was a Jesuit priest.

Jesuits were members of The Society of Jesus, a religious order in the Roman Catholic Church. Jesuit means "Soldier of Christ," a name given by the founder of the order, Saint Ignatius of Loyola, who was a soldier—actually a knight—before becoming a priest. Father Oliver functioned in his order as a traveling priest, in constant motion, meeting and serving the needs of other priests in his order in any way his pledge to poverty would allow.

He was in New York when he got the phone call from a mutual friend of his and Ruby's, another childhood friend, telling him of the tragic accident that had killed Carl and nearly killed Connie—and may yet. He left his duties in New York and immediately sought out Ruby and Henry to comfort them in any way he could. When he arrived in Chilton, he was met by his old friend and driven to Ruby and Henry's house, carrying a small suitcase with contents fully consistent with his pledge to poverty. He dressed simply, with black trousers and a Roman collar tab shirt under his very heavy winter overcoat. Within the first hour of his arrival, Ruby and Henry drove him to St. Agnes to see Connie.

When Father Oliver walked into Connie's room behind Ruby and Henry, he saw Connie beyond them and audibly gasped. "Oh, God Almighty," he volunteered while restraining himself in his demeanor, "what has become of your lamb?" With a quick shrug of his shoulders, his heavy overcoat slipped from his shoulders. "We pray that your blessing will get her through this perilous time." He wasn't prepared to see Connie in her present state, so unrecognizable, so cauterized in bandages. He begged Jesus, Mary, and Joseph to help him find the wisdom to provide the comfort these three souls must surely need.

Father Oliver was told that many more surgeries lay ahead, but for now, her recovery would go undisturbed for several weeks while she was confined to bed for an indefinite time. Her comatose state made the next step nearly unidentifiable. As soon as he got to her bedside, he knew what he had to do. He folded his coat into a neat square and, placing it on the floor as a kneeling pad, he fell to his knees and began praying aloud, as Ruby and Henry stood a half step behind him. "Dear Lord," he solemnly began, placing his hand on Connie's exposed hand, which was at her side and held in place by a safety strap:

> *"I praise and thank you for all the graces you have bestowed upon us and the strength you have given Ruby and Henry to face this difficulty. I humbly prostrate myself before you and ask that you look down on Connie with compassion. Come to her assistance in this great need, that she may receive the help of heaven in all her suffering, and bring her back to us in every way healthy. Despise not my poor prayer and let not my trust be in vain. For my small and humble part, I will hold onto Connie as long as it takes for her to come back to us. I ask your blessing in my unswerving commitment from this moment on. Amen."*

Ruby and Henry followed his "Amen" with their own, in unison, softly, and knew this was all out of their hands. They were devout Catholics and knew then that they had to put their trust in God.

Father Oliver turned to face Ruby and Henry without letting go of Connie's hand and said, "I will stay here and pray for her and not let go of her hand until she comes back to us.

My prayers are for you too, that you may get through this difficult time. You can expect to find me here, whenever you visit her." With that, he returned to praying on his knees, this time in silence, and bowed his head close to Connie's hand, the one he held in his own hand, while his other hand held onto the small silver cross that hung from a chain around his neck. It was his duty; he was, after all, a Soldier of Christ.

"Thank you, Father Oliver," Henry said softly. Ruby repeated Henry's words. Then, together, they left the room in silence and gratitude for this man's gift.

Five hours later, close to the midnight hour, Father Oliver rose from his knees and walked slowly, stiff from his supplications, down the hall a few rooms to relieve himself in the men's room. When he returned to Connie's room, he pulled a chair up to her bedside, where he entwined his hand in her safety strap, took her exposed hand in his once again, and proceeded to fall asleep. In the morning, he would go to his knees again, in a full day of prayer. He would live this pattern every day until Connie came back from wherever she was, just as he had promised God, for however long it would take.

There are people in this world that make a difference, perhaps many more than we acknowledge. As all of us move through life, we hear, almost daily, the news of people doing heroic things, like saving babies from burning vehicles, jumping on subway tracks to pull someone out of the path of danger, rescuing flood victims from swift currents, and countless other courageous acts of rescue. The media thrives on these public heroes, and we are all thankful for them. However, let us not forget that heroic acts don't always require that we put our lives at risk. Every individual can make a difference, if they want to, simply by being there for someone else.

Sometimes no act is required at all; sometimes just the offer of "being there for you" and meaning it makes all the difference in someone's life. We all should try to be that meaningful person. But I digress.

CHAPTER TWENTY-TWO

It had been two weeks since the accident. Connie was still in a coma, a deep unconsciousness, in the intensive care unit of St. Agnes hospital in Fond du Lac, Wisconsin. It was Saturday, December 28, 1946. The snow was higher than ever, and the week was one of the coldest weeks many could remember in many years.

alive....................maybe..…...........
....…..
.....................................…........not...sure.............................…......
...............................…..
...................................…..it was all
nothingness...…....................
....…........................
.............nothingness defined by emptiness, a nothingness of
everything that was..….…......
...................................…..
.............................…...
.............nothing..…....................
....
......................a forever of nothingness......................
...…...
....

……without dimension of any kind……………………………
………………………………………………………………..
………………………………………..………………………
……………unless infinity was a dimension…………………...
…………………………….…………………………………
……………………………………………………..……………
……………………………….nothing……………………………
………………………………………………………..…………
nothing………………………………………………....………
……………………………………………………………………
…....………nothing…………………….…………..……………
…..………………………………………………………………
……………………………………………………………....…
infinite nothingness in a place that was timeless………………
……………………………………………………………………..
………………………………………………………………………
………then whatever consciousness she had…………………..
…………………………….…………………………………
…………………………………………..disappeared……..……..…

CHAPTER TWENTY-THREE

It had been two months since the accident. It was Valentine's Day, 1947. Connie was still in a coma, still in the intensive care unit in St. Agnes Hospital.

This day was much like the first sixty days of their visits. Ruby and Henry walked into her room. Connie was slowly healing. Her body cast had been removed the week before. The swelling was down. Her color had improved—from the purples and blacks to yellows of deep contusions to a ghostly pale, almost translucent white. There was now some resemblance to life, if one looked carefully. Scars ran like red zippers, creating a map-like patchwork across her face where the glass from the windshield had shredded her face. She had lost her left eye, and in its place, was a bulbous ping-pong ball sized dressing holding a place for the arrival of a prosthetic eye—although no one could be sure if that would even work.

Father Oliver was at her bedside, on his knees, holding her hand in one hand and his silver cross in the other, just as he had been doing since his first appearance. When he rotated his head to greet Ruby and Henry, was when his weight loss was most apparent. He had dropped about ten pounds from his slight frame since that first day at the hospital. The lay staff and the nuns of St. Agnes did their best to provide him with comfort during his Crusade. He asked for very little and professed a comfort level that he couldn't possibly have felt, except for the fact that all of his attention these many weeks had been on Connie's recovery and not on himself. He hadn't given up hope; he just prayed even harder and spent even more time on his knees.

When they saw each other, Ruby greeted him first in almost a whisper, "Hello Father Oliver," she said, speaking for Henry as well, as a habit they had slipped into. Henry just nodded.

"Hello Ruby. Hello, Henry," he replied. It was evident from his expression that he had no news. "I wish I could share some good news with you," he added, "other than that she's still with us. And, we can be thankful that her healing continues." He paused, wanting to sound upbeat, but Connie's silence in her comatose state was almost oppressive. She was so still, alive on a support system, without a flicker of life, unless you could count the incessant hissing and beeping of the equipment in the room. Father Oliver turned to face Connie again and spoke to her: "Connie, we know you are with us and you will come back to us. God will answer our prayers, and I will stay with you every step of the way until you return to us."

Ruby moved into the room and stepped to the opposite side of the bed from Father Oliver but closer to the head of the bed. Henry stayed at the side next to Father Oliver, head high and opposite Ruby.

Henry's eyes locked with Father Oliver's in an exchange of many human emotions, not the least of which were sympathy, gratitude, pain, compassion and, of course, love. "Thank you, Father Oliver, thank you," he said. "It means a lot to us, a lot," he repeated, "that you're here. I'm sure you know that." Father Oliver looked Henry in his sorrowful eyes and nodded. He understood perfectly. Henry had thanked him in this manner every day.

Ruby leaned over into the space above Connie's face, tears in her eyes, gazing with that special kind of love that is only and truly motherly. She slowly moved her left hand to Connie's face and, with the gentlest of touches, stroked her forehead and then her cheeks over and over again and talked to her. "Connie," she began, "please, Connie, come back to us." She paused, so choked up with hope, love, and what she fought off as despair. The odds seemed to be so much against her little girl. She didn't know how anyone could get through this ordeal. "Connie," she continued, "you're getting better every day, and you will make it through all this suffering. I know you will." She paused again before continuing with her soothing words, mindless of anyone else's presence. It was surely a most private moment between a mother and her daughter. Both Henry and Father Oliver were deeply moved by this expression of such great love, as they watched this maternal communication.

"Connie," Ruby whispered, "you remember how much your father loved you, don't you?" she asked, as if having a conversation. "Remember what he said to you whenever you fell down and scraped your knee? He told me how he had to hold himself back from picking you up in his arms when tears were streaming down your little cheeks and you looked to him for comfort... He didn't come to you right away so that you'd know you had the strength in yourself to stand up and get through a bad moment. He loved you so much, and he'd tell you right now if he could... You can get through this bad moment, Connie. You can do it, but you have to do it yourself." For a full minute, in the silence of the room, Ruby gently massaged Connie's face and then carefully pushed

Connie's blonde hair back from her face, leaned over, and let a soft kiss linger on her forehead.

For the next hour, Ruby and Henry sat in the two chairs in the room while Father Oliver continued to pray on his knees. All three of them prayed, and Connie never moved.

Father Oliver's commitment to spend his conscious hours on his knees at Connie's bedside, holding her hand and praying for her recovery for as long as it would take was a remarkable expression of faith, which was evident to all who entered Connie's hospital room. It was a commitment that he had made to God and to Connie that was unbounded with respect to time. Surely, he had no idea how long she would be unconscious, lost in a coma, when he first dropped to his knees. Was he thinking her condition would change within a day or two and she would move back into life or into the afterlife he believed in? That cannot be known. Had he realized that she could be in a coma for years, which would require an unfathomable personal commitment on his part? That cannot be known. What was his state of being, as week after week and month after month passed? That cannot be known. What was he thinking in regard to the other responsibilities he must have had elsewhere in his duties as a Jesuit priest? That cannot be known.

There's so much about life that is beyond our knowledge and understanding, so much beyond the known. But he made this commitment and stuck to it. What a truly remarkable statement about faith! He held onto his faith. And he held onto my mother's hand. Maybe that's why she never let go of life. But I digress.

CHAPTER TWENTY-FOUR

It had been four months since the accident. It was April 14, 1947. Connie was still in a coma. Ruby and Henry entered Connie's hospital room, this time in the afternoon. They stood at her bedside and talked briefly with Father Oliver before arranging the room's two chairs in a way that would allow them see Connie's good eye, even though it was closed, as it had been since the accident. Ruby and Henry must have glanced at Connie's closed eye every minute. It was the focal point of their love, and they prayed it would suddenly open, like the flick of a light switch, and—lo and behold—Connie's light would bring joy to a room where there had been none for many months.

..........yes..................alive......was that what it was?.........
.........................…..…........
...........................…..…..........
there was always so much nothingness.............it was..........
...............................…..
........................…..everywhere..........…....................................
................................…...........................…..................................
...........and she was in the middle of this..........................
..................................…..
.....nothingness......................................…..........................
...................but this time it seemed a little thicker.........

…………………………………………………………
………………………..but only so briefly……………………..
…………………………………………………………
…………………………………………so…..briefly………….
……………………………………………………...………..………
she wanted to move on, on to some new place…………a better
place……………………………………………………...…..
…………………………………………………………
………………………but she couldn't………………………
…………………………………………………………
..…………………….she had to stay………………………
…………………………………………………………
……Connie……………………………………………………..
…………………………………………………………
…………………again……………………………...………
…………………………………………………………
…………Connie…she heard her name, yes, her name……….
……………………………...……………………………..
…………………………………………………………
…………………………she had to stay………………...……
…………………………………………………………
…………………something was holding onto her…………….
…………………………………………………………
…………………………………………………………
…...something wouldn't let her go…………………………..
…………………………………………………………
…something she couldn't define was holding onto her…….
………………………………………………...…..
……………..……and it wouldn't let go………………………
…………………………………………...………..……
…………………………………………………………

…………………………………….then nothing again………..
……………………………………………………………………
………………too-ra-loo……………………………………….
……………………………………………………………………
…….nothing……………………………………...…...………..
…………………………………………...……nothing…………..
…………………………….……………………………………
……………………………….…………………………………
………………….....…………………………………………….
….. someone was holding onto her ………..……………………..
……………………………….……………………………………
……………………………….then whatever consciousness she had
……….disappeared.………………………………………………..

CHAPTER TWENTY FIVE

It had been six months since the accident. It was June 14, 1947. Connie was still in a coma. Ruby and Henry had just entered Connie's hospital room. They stood at her bedside and talked briefly with Father Oliver before he returned to the solitude of his prayers, as was his habit. Ruby and Henry pulled up chairs to Connie's bedside and made themselves as comfortable as they could for their daily visit. Sometimes they came in the morning; sometimes in the afternoon.

Connie's physical condition continued to improve with the passage of each week, although her road to full recovery would be a long one—if she recovered. Her jaw was no longer wired shut, but it was heavily bandaged from on-going mini-surgeries. Her legs were still in a plaster cradle, and the bones were healing through several surgeries. She had healed quite a bit and no longer had any bruises. Even her scars, which had been everywhere, no longer looked like angry welts. No one had ever given up hope. They told themselves that she could snap out of it any minute—bingo!—just like that!

When Ruby and Henry visited, they spoke to her directly, as if she were fully involved in their conversation, taking turns telling her how many of her friends were asking about her and sharing their news, while wanting to believe that Connie could hear everything despite her inactivity. Dr. von Hoerner encouraged them to talk to her, and they did. Every day since their first time with her, they spoke with her. It gave them hope. Sometimes Ruby would sing to Connie. The song she sang most often was "Too Ra Loo Ra Loo Ral," an Irish lullaby. It was a song that became a hit when Bing Crosby sang it in "Going My Way" in 1944. Ruby liked it; she thought it was soothing:

> Over in Killarney,
> Many years ago,
> Me mither sang a song to me
> In tones so sweet and low.
> Just a simple little ditty,
> In her good ould Irish way,
> And I'd give the world if she could sing
> That song to me this day.
> Too-ra-loo-ra-loo-ral,
> Too-ra-loo-ra-li,
> Too-ra-loo-ra-loo-ral,
> Hush, now don't you cry!
> Too-ra-loo-ra-loo-ral,
> Too-ra-loo-ra-li,
> Too-ra-loo-ra-loo-ral,
> That's an Irish lullaby.
>
> Oft, in dreams I wander
> To that cot again,
> I feel her arms a huggin' me
> As when she held me then.
> And I hear her voice a humin'
> To me as in days or yore,

When she used to rock me fast asleep
Outside the cabin door.
Too-ra-loo-ra-loo-ral,
Too-ra-loo-ra-li,
Too-ra-loo-ra-loo-ral,
Hush, now don't you cry!
Too-ra-loo-ra-loo-ral,
Too-ra-loo-ra-li,
Too-ra-loo-ra-loo-ral,
That's an Irish lullaby.

the nothingness was gone…………………………………………
…………………………………………...fading………………
…………………………………too-ra-loo……………..……………
……………...once it was everywhere……………now it was…
…………………...nowhere………………..…it was gone….…..
………………………………………………………………………
…………… someone was holding her hand………………...…....
…………………………………that was the feeling……………
………………………………………………..……………………
someone had been holding her hand…………………………….
……………she thought that's what kept her from leaving….
…………..……………..from going to that infinite……………..
………place…………………………………………………………
…………………………………it wasn't her time to go…………
…………………………………too-ra-loo…………………..…………
………………………………………Connie…………..…………
…someone said her name………………………………………...
………………...............…..her mother said her name…………it was
her mother's voice…...………………………………………………

....…............
.......too-ra-loo-ra-loo-ral...............................too-ra-loo-ra-li...…...
.................and Henry's voice..
....…....................................
...............Henry was her stepfather......she knew that.........
.......the nothingness was gone...…....
.................her hand was warm, in someone else's hand.........
....
....but whose hand was it?..........
.....................was it her mother's?.......................................
....…........no, her mother was by her
other hand............it wasn't Henry's hand.......................
....
Henry's hand wasn't soft...................…....this was soft and dry
....…..…
..............................the hand felt good................…...........
.........but it was enough..…......
....
........someone was holding onto her....she knew that now......
...…..
.... she squeezed it, but it was all she could do.........
..............................then whatever consciousness she had
disappeared...
....…...............then...............
it came right back!...

Father Oliver's entire face contorted, and he gasped as if he were a man fighting for his last gasp of air, so startled was he when Connie squeezed his hand. The sensation was electrifying, as if ten thousand volts surged into his heart. He cried out, "Oh, my God! God has answered our prayers!" He looked to Ruby, then Henry, then back to Ruby. "Ruby, Henry, Connie just squeezed my hand! She squeezed my hand! Jesus, Mary, and Joseph! She squeezed my hand!"

Ruby and Henry jumped to their feet and moved to Connie's face, expecting... expecting what? Maybe she would open her eye and see them. Long seconds of silence passed. Nothing happened. Connie didn't move again. Henry pulled back from the bed and ran out of the room, crying out, "I'll get Doc!" Ruby and Father Oliver could hear Henry's voice fading down the hall as he ran for help, "Doctor von Hoerner! Doctor von Hoerner!"

Not five minutes passed when Henry ran back into the room. Dr. von Hoerner was right behind him, along with the floor's duty nurse. Henry charged into the room, looking so hopeful, like a kid on Christmas morning, surely expecting to see Connie sitting up in bed and chatting away.

"Well?" Henry demanded, looking at Father Oliver, then Ruby, then back to Father Oliver, then back to Ruby. He could see no visible change in Connie. "What happened? Is she back? Is she back?"

"Henry," Ruby said, admonishing him, "calm down." Then Ruby turned to face Dr. von Hoerner while Father Oliver deferred to her as the bearer of the momentous news. "Doctor, Connie squeezed Father Oliver's hand!"

"Is this true, Father?" von Hoerner asked, hopeful but cautious about not jumping to conclusions."

"Yes, Docter, yes," replied Father Oliver, who was now standing. Connie squeezed my hand. I know she did. I've been waiting six months for a sign. I couldn't have imagined it."

"I believe you, Father. It might be something," he replied

as he moved to the other side of the bed, to the far side from the door. He placed his hand on Connie's neck to check the pulse from her carotid artery. A pulse registered, and he noted to himself that it was strong. At that moment, no one said anything. Ruby and Henry were holding their breath with the possibilities. Father Oliver was looking up to the ceiling, clearly in an intense prayer, his folded prayerful hands shaking visibly, with fingertips pressed to his lips. Then Dr. von Hoerner gently moved his left hand upward to Connie's good eye and, with a soft touch, lifted her eyelid to check her pupil, hoping he'd see more than the motionless, dilated pupil that he had seen every day for the past six months. When her lid came up, Connie looked right at him, into his eyes.

The moments that Dr. von Hoerner stood over Connie were so quiet that you could hear a pin drop in the room. Ruby and Henry and Father Oliver held their breath, exercising excruciating patience for the next words out of Dr. von Hoerner's mouth, as he leaned over Connie within a foot of her face.

He spoke to her, softly and lovingly. "Hello, Connie," he said. "We've missed you!"

Ruby nearly fainted; she collapsed like a dropped dish towel in her chair. Henry yelled out, "Oh, my God! Connie's back! Thank you, Lord, thank you!" and thrust his arms upward. Father Oliver fell to his knees and kissed his silver cross. Dr. von Hoerner stood tall. It was the only outcome he had let himself contemplate.

Dr. von Hoerner was already thinking about putting a plan in motion for Connie's rehabilitation. And he had something else to do—something that required him to be alone with Connie. For the immediate moment, he asked everyone to go home and let Connie rest and give her some time to orient herself. It wasn't easy for Ruby and Henry or, for that matter, Father Oliver to leave, but they followed Dr. von Hoerner's advice.

The three of them left the room, speechless in happiness, looking at each other with faces that made up a collage of smiles, tears, lip-biting, and sighs of joy. But most of all, they were high with the lightheadedness of relief because the fog that had enveloped for Connie for six months had finally lifted. Ten minutes later, in Henry's car on the way back to Chilton, all three were talking all at once and couldn't stop talking, so great was their elation.

Later that day, well after the dinner hour and well after Ruby and Henry had made countless telephone calls to friends and family, they reflected on what they had told everyone, and the most commonly uttered phrase in the telling was, "It's a miracle!"

No one knows how to explain a patient's return from a coma, nor what the trigger was for Connie's recovery to consciousness, nor if it was a single trigger or multiple ones or some unique formulation of triggers. Was it the medical treatment and the committed attention and care of Dr. von Hoerner and his dedicated staff? Was it the constant human contact and love provided daily by three individuals? Was it divine intervention? Was it an Irish lullaby? Was it simply that nature needed time to heal Connie's wounds? I say, it doesn't make any difference because the outcome was what everyone had hoped for. There was lots of rejoicing in the knowledge that Connie had come back! How great it is to know that the human spirit, for whatever reason, can overcome so much adversity! But I digress.

CHAPTER TWENTY-SIX

While Ruby and Henry and Father Oliver were driving back to Chilton late that afternoon, Dr. von Hoerner stood at Connie's bedside and talked to her. He knew she was conscious, even though she hadn't opened her good eye. He was faced with a dilemma. Exactly how conscious she was, was difficult to assess, but he couldn't take the chance that she would be suffering over not knowing or understanding her situation, specifically, why she was in the hospital, how long she had been there, and what it all meant. He had to tell her some things, even if they would hurt her to hear them. He made the decision that it would be worse, and possibly terrifying, for her to be alone without any understanding of her circumstances. But when was the right time to have that discussion, he wondered? He looked at her heart rate on the monitor and could see that it had risen a bit. This was actually a good sign, as it indicated some responsiveness to her environment. He would watch it closely.

Dr. von Hoerner leaned over her face again and lifted her eyelid. Her pupil quickly contracted, adjusting to the light once again. She was looking at him. She hadn't lifted her lid on her own—maybe that would take some time, he thought to himself. He pulled back his thumb and let her lid naturally fall into place; her eye was closed once again.

"Connie," he said upon embracing her exposed hand on his

side of the bed, "give my hand one quick squeeze if you can hear me."

He waited.

Connie wanted to respond.

Twenty seconds later, Connie gave Dr. von Hoerner what he wanted: a quick squeeze, although its weakness registered with the doctor.

"That's good, Connie—real good." He paused with indecision. He wondered if he should take it further or let her rest until tomorrow, which would give her a little more time. He wanted her to open her own eyelid. Maybe another day is what she needed. He decided to let her rest. "Connie, you get some more rest. Tomorrow will come soon enough," he spoke in a soothing voice. "We'll know more tomorrow." He squeezed her hand and reached for her chart to note the experience with a gladdened heart. She didn't respond. Maybe she had fallen asleep.

Dr. von Hoerner made a short entry on her chart: "First day patient is responsive. No change in protocol yet," he scribbled. He returned the chart to the basket at the foot of the bed and walked out of the room with a lighter step in his stride than he had felt in six months.

He believed that Connie could hear him, but he would be very careful in his choice of words when he spoke to her. He hoped fervently that she would understand his words.

There was no known explanation for Connie's return. Apparently she had recovered, at least to a basic degree, from her traumatic head injuries, although whether or not there was any permanent brain injury had not yet been determined. Clearly, Dr. von Hoerner was encouraged by what he saw. We will never know where she had gone in the six months she had been comatose and how or why she had regained consciousness. There are places in the mind we simply don't know about. But I digress.

CHAPTER TWENTY-SEVEN

………………...…….she was alone………so quiet…………...

…..……………………………………………………………..

………………………she wiggled her fingers on one hand…………

…………then the other………………………………………………

the nothingness was gone. …it had faded away………………..

……….…………….. gone………………………………………..

…………she had looked into his eyes…………………………

………………………….…she knew him………………………

……they talked…. or something…………………she heard his

words……………………………………………………………...

she wanted to hear more……….but so tired…………………...

…………………….so tired……..tired……………………...…

………………….……she couldn't move for some reason……...

………there must be a reason……………………………….…

she knew she was in a bed…………in a hospital……………..

……………………………………………………..……………

………………………..and then she knew why……………...

…..a tear formed in her eye and made a run for it……………..

………………………………….it was for Carl……………...

………………………………she knew he was gone…..

…another tear…….it slid down her cheek……………………...

……….on the same path as the last one……….she felt that…..

………………………………………………………………...

…as she remembered….he was looking at her as they………...

as they..…........
.................what?.........as they......flew............................…....
................as they flew together......toward death..............
..........death........................…........she could see him at that
final moment..….......
......................he was looking at her.........................…....
..................Carl..
...........................…...she was alive......................oh....
...........God...oh God..…....
Carl is gone........................dear God.........................…..
God...no...no.............no...….
...................my baby!..................my baby!...........................
......what about.......my baby?..
.........another tear...and......
another..…....
......no answer...................and then a new nothingness......
.......a different nothingness..…..
...........softer.........warm......the terror was gone..............…..
.....this was the nothingness that sleep brings....................…...
.......................she embraced it....she didn't want..........…..
....…...
.....she didn't want to remember............…......didn't.....want to.....
........remember...….......

CHAPTER TWENTY-EIGHT

Sometime in the middle of that night, in a room that was very dark, but for a sliver of light that was under the door to her room but too small to provide any illumination, Connie woke up. She felt herself—whatever it was that she was—and she was no longer feeling nothing. She felt alive again. She breathed deeply. She could feel her heart beat. She could feel her fingers. She wasn't sure she wiggled her toes, although she tried. She couldn't see them, and they didn't feel particularly part of her. Not everything felt right, but she felt right in a way that she hadn't felt forever.

Then she opened her eye.

She cast her vision around the darkness of her room. She felt hollow in the same place on the left side, and her bandage in that location seemed to reach into the center of her head. Her right eye absorbed the darkness, all of it. She looked around and locked onto a very faint outline, a pin stripe of soft light around the top half of the room's door; its bottom half was not in her range. She could see. She could see what she knew was light, although it was barely discernible. She knew that the rectilinear halo on the door was created by the light in the hallway, the hallway of the hospital she was in. Earlier, in searing light, she had recognized Dr. von Hoerner when he'd stood over her. This meant she must be in St. Agnes in Fond du Lac. She could see a different darkness, framed by the outline of the frame of the room's only window.

Yes, this was a different kind of darkness, the darkness of night, but she could see it. She could make out small soft shadows moving outside her window, swaying... leaves? Leaves! She could see they were leaves of trees!... That didn't make sense. It was winter... the middle of December. But— no—it couldn't be December. Those were certainly leaves, caught in the moonlight or... or maybe burnished by a streetlamp that was beyond the window's view. "Winter must be over," she concluded. "Was it spring? Was it summer?" In so much darkness, it was hard to tell much of anything. She wasn't scared by the darkness—any of it. She could see it, and it meant she was alive.

"But," a memory suddenly broke into her thoughts, coming to her like a bolt of lightning, "... but... but... my baby?" she asked herself. What, she wondered, was the answer to that question? Despair moved in under the protection of the darkness of the room. It was ponderous, and it parked on her bed, weighing tons and big and threatening, like a truck about to run her over. And there was nothing she could do about it.

"Mind, be still," she told herself over and over again, "I don't know anything for sure. I just don't know. Maybe I'll learn something in the morning. I can wait. Yes, I can wait till the morning." She closed her eye and then, with the help of the sedatives being fed through a tube into her system, she drifted off to sleep, as the truck drove away and disappeared into the darkness.

The hope that was once so infinitesimally small, like the flicker of a distant candle, was growing, and now the flame's heat could be felt for the first time in a long time. The cold of the emptiness was gone. As a kid, when I was feeling down, for whatever reason—for what probably were silly reasons in retrospect—my mom would say to me, "The day is darkest just before the dawn." It helped me to know that. It gave me the confidence that things would look better eventually, but surely I didn't know when I was so young why she attached so much meaning to those words. Now I do. But I digress.

CHAPTER TWENTY-NINE

With the rising of the sun on what promised to be a beautiful summer day in June in central Wisconsin, Ruby and Henry pulled into the hospital's parking lot. It wasn't easy leaving Connie the day before after hearing the great, great news that she had come out of her coma at long last, but Dr. von Hoerner, they felt, had spoken wisely. With a night of sleep behind them, although fitful with the anticipation of seeing the awakened Connie, they were ready to spend the entire day at her side.

At the doorway of Connie's room, she looked exactly as she had looked for the last six months, eerily still and lifeless, although with a lot less gauze and bandages, plaster, and IV drips. Something was different, however, and the sunlight flowing into the room through the room's only window masked the difference at first, but the mask didn't hold up under scrutiny. Connie had more color to her. Gone was the pasty, white, translucence that had defined her being during the deep, deep sleep of the past six months.

Ruby and Henry slowly and quietly stepped farther into the room, wanting to be careful not to disturb Connie's slumber. Their appearances had changed too. They were almost giddy from the massive amount of hope that was flowing through their being. Emanations of their love and their sudden vitality over Connie's return filled the room and washed over Connie's tiny, thin frame, a frame that had become diminutive. Even so, Connie definitely looked better, even though she didn't stir. Ruby and Henry silently slid the two old chairs that they had been sitting in for months and months to Connie's bedside once again, for nearly the two hundredth time. They could see, for the first time in such a long, long time, that Connie looked alive.

Two hours passed as they waited for Dr. von Hoerner's expected appearance at eight that morning. In that period, one of the nurses silently stepped in, checked the equipment, the drips, and then signed the chart with what could only have been encouraging words and departed with a big smile. Like everyone on the floor, she had heard the news in every detail that was available.

The other visit was by a St. Agnes nun, Sister Mary LaVinia Philothea, who floated into the room shortly after that, nodded to Ruby and Henry, went to the foot of Connie's bed, made the sign of the cross, bowed her head, and commenced with a silent prayer. This was part of her daily ritual and had been since Connie's arrival in intensive care. Right after Sister Philothea signed off her prayer, Henry thought he saw her do a bit of a double-take when she noticed the empty space at Connie's bedside, the space that had been perpetually occupied by Father Oliver, kneeling or not. It did seem funny that he wasn't there, but he couldn't be. At dawn, when Ruby and Henry had left for the hospital, Father Oliver had left for New York to return to his unfinished work there. He felt his work was finished in Chilton. Then, Sister Philothea left on the same current of air that had carried her in, and just as silently as when she had entered.

Ruby and Henry waited in silence. Henry looked at his

watch, then he put his wrist in front of Ruby's face so that she could see the time. It was eight o'clock, exactly. After Ruby looked at the face of his watch, she looked at Henry's face, at which point, Dr. von Hoerner walked into the room and headed directly to Connie's bedside, the one on the far side of the bed.

"Good morning, Ruby," he said halfway into the room, and in stride, added, "Good morning, Henry. And," he paused a beat, "good morning, Connie!" He went right to Connie and, as if on cue, Connie opened her eye and met Dr. von Hoerner's eyes as he stood at her side. "Good to see you awake, Connie." He let himself break out of his professional demeanor and smiled, putting the back of his hand tenderly to her cheek and then slowly withdrew it, still smiling.

Ruby and Henry were already to their feet and gathered themselves behind him as closely as possible, which put the threesome into Connie's line of vision. Dr. von Hoerner took a step back to let them move in closer.

"Oh, Connie," Ruby said, "Oh, my little girl—you've come back to us!" Ruby carefully cupped Connie's face in her hands and kissed her forehead over and over again, dropping several tears onto Connie's face before regaining her composure, which wasn't at all easy to do, given the miraculous circumstances. Henry put his hands on top of Connie's exposed hand on that side of the bedside, surprised suddenly by the warmth in her hand—warmth that he hadn't felt in all those months.

Connie looked at both of them lovingly because that is all and everything she felt at the moment. She, too, shed a tear that quickly trickled to the base of her ear and then disappeared under the back edge of the bandage that covered her jaw.

Henry moved in to kiss her as well. She was his little girl

too, in every way, although he wasn't her biological father. His heart was bursting with joy that she was back, and his eyes filled with tears too. Henry moved closer to Connie, and just as he moved his lips to her forehead, his tear dropped onto her cheek, just below her eye and mingled with one of her own. Connie inhaled his fragrance, the fragrance of the cigars that he loved for so many years, a distinctive fragrance that was inseparable from Henry's being.

For a fleeting moment, she felt she was at home and she was a little girl, but that moment quickly dissolved as Ruby and Henry stepped back, making way for Dr. von Hoerner's return to the forefront of her vision. She looked at von Hoerner, and all of the heart-heavy questions she'd had in the still of the night rushed back. She couldn't move her jaw yet, so she couldn't talk. She couldn't move anything yet, except her fingers and possibly her toes. She wasn't sure about her toes. She looked to Dr. von Hoerner to lead the way with answers to her questions. Hopefully, he'd give them to her.

Dr. von Hoerner grasped Connie's right hand in his right hand. His other hand was empty—he didn't need the chart to remind him of her status or of what she had gone through. "Connie," Dr. von Hoerner began, "I believe you can understand what we've been saying, but to make sure, please squeeze my hand if you can hear me and understand me." He didn't have to wait a second to feel Connie's squeeze. This was a good sign. It made him think that her mental capacity was undiminished, and whatever fear he had about serious brain damage quickly disappeared. He continued, "I'm going to ask you several questions, and I want you to squeeze my hand once if the answer is yes and twice if your answer is no. Okay?"

Connie squeezed once.

"You were in a terrible car accident last December." He spoke slowly, in an even tempo, careful in choosing his words. "That," he continued after skipping a beat, "was six months ago. Today is June 15, 1947. It is a miracle that you survived." This he said modestly, as Ruby and Henry knew how much he had put into saving Connie's life and caring for her every minute of her ordeal. For his next question, he wanted to be careful because he didn't know if Connie knew that Carl was dead, and he chose to probe her understanding before to decide what he could say or not say. "Do you remember the accident at all?"

Connie squeezed once.

At this point, Dr. Hoerner had to ask if she knew that Carl had been killed. Had she indicated "no" to the previous question, then he probably would have put that information in abeyance. If she remembered anything, as she had indicated that she did, then the stress—or the suspense—of not knowing for sure about his status, he felt, should be dealt with immediately. If she knew the truth—that Carl was dead—then the question would be moot. Von Hoerner moved forward, exercising an acute sensitivity in bedside manner, which had been carefully cultivated for over thirty years. "Do you know about Carl?"

Connie squeezed once. A tear ran down her cheek.

"I'm sorry, Connie," he said, "deeply sorry." At this point Ruby went to the other side of the bed and gingerly held Connie's left hand. Henry remained behind and to the right of Dr. von Hoerner, still in Connie's line of sight. Connie could see Ruby when she glanced to her left, which she had already done a couple of times. There would be more emotional pain, and it would be extensive momentarily, he was sure of that.

"Connie," he said lowering his voice, "did you know you were pregnant at the time of the accident?"

Connie squeezed once. Another tear and another after that in quick succession ran down her cheek. She closed her eye, trying to prepare herself for what she now expected the doctor to tell her. She knew the truth—it had come to her in the dark—but she needed to hear it from him to give it wings.

"You lost the baby, but I'm guessing you know that, don't you?"

Connie squeezed once. Her eye remained closed, but that didn't stop another tear from running down her cheek.

Dr. von Hoerner looked at Ruby and saw the tears running down her face as well. "I'm so sorry. This is so difficult... but it is necessary to get on with the healing." Connie's eye remained closed.

"Are you with me, Connie?" von Hoerner asked.

Connie squeezed once, but not right away.

"It is my duty, however it saddens me, to tell you now about the extent of your injuries, at least with regard to your condition at the moment. Over these past six months, you have been a very good healer and made it through many of your injuries, especially internal ones, although miraculously, with a strong prognosis for no permanent damage to your vital organs, and you've made it through many surgeries. It appears you've gotten through this period without debilitating head injuries, even though the trauma to your head was enormous. Part of the head trauma, included the loss of your left eye...." He paused for everyone's benefit, as this list, which had only just begun, was already taking a toll on everyone's emotions. "I've already talked to specialists who can help you. They are confident that you'll be able to get a good prosthesis, and the orbital damage can be repaired with some success. It has already healed quite a bit. Are you with me, Connie?"

Connie squeezed once. She didn't know that she had lost an eye. This was news, and it explained the hollowness that she had been feeling on the left side of her face. Before she could dwell on it, Dr. von Hoerner was speaking again.

"You've been on a feeding tube for the past six months. This has caused considerable weight loss and atrophy of your muscles, but you will likely return to your normal weight once you are out and about. It will be another month or so before you will be able to eat any solid foods. Your jaw was traumatized with numerous breaks, and considerable dental work is ahead of you. Even so, as I said, you've been a great healer. A lot of progress has been made in this area." He paused again and then said, "Are you with me, Connie?"

Connie squeezed once. She opened her eye and looked at von Hoerner. He took this as a good sign, that she had the inner strength for him to continue.

"While you lie here with a cast supporting your pelvic region and both of your legs, the stability of your left leg, in particular, is still in doubt. It was severely damaged—almost severed—but re-attachment seems to have worked, at least for the time being. We can't be sure at this point, but it appears that you have severe bilateral leg peripheral nerve injury and, for the present time, there's a likelihood that you won't be able to walk." On this note, von Hoerner glanced at Henry. "There are certain therapies we had to put off while you were in a coma. Now that you're conscious, we can look into these possibilities. However, I think you should know that recovery is... well, frankly... the prognosis isn't good. You will leave this hospital in a wheelchair... and... may be confined to one the rest of your life, but we can't be sure of that yet." Von Hoerner sighed and ran his fingers over his eyes as if they were tired, but he was actually wiping away the moisture of budding tears caused by this news. This prognosis was tough to deliver, and he had to sublimate his memories of the young Connie Ortlieb, Chilton's golden girl, who could outrun the boys at any distance and climb higher in trees than anyone else. "Are you with me, Connie?"

He waited for the squeeze. None. Connie was looking at Ruby with a look of a lost little girl who wondered if she'd ever find her way home. Dr. von Hoerner thought he saw a little terror mixed in with that look, as well. He couldn't be sure, as he waited for Connie to respond. Several moments passed before he repeated himself, "Connie, are you with me?"

Connie squeezed once and looked upward to the ceiling, with a gaze that was meant for infinite space. She hoped she wouldn't hear any more from Dr. von Hoerner, but there was more to come; she could tell. What other news could he possibly deliver that could make her feel any worse than she already felt? The weight of despair had returned. And it was growing, and it was already bigger than a truck.

"Your pelvic area and legs went through a lot. The tibia and fibula—you know, the big upper and lower bones in both legs—were broken in half. Both of them have a total of ten to twelve pins in them to support the bone structure but, as I said, it appears the bones have done quite a bit of healing in the past several months. That's actually the good news. The same with your pelvis—the damage to it will also present some complications in your rehabilitative efforts to walk again, but the fractures appear to have healed as well, although the decrease in mineralization—you know, calcium in particular—

from being sedentary for so long has been extensive. Your bone mass has diminished considerably."

He continued after a deep, slow breath.

"The damage was extensive and, we think, may include considerable nerve damage below the pelvic region. Let me say something about that nerve damage," he continued, "We don't know if the nerves were transected or not, you know, destroyed or not. If they were severed, you might not be able to walk again. If the nerves are merely injured—for example, crushed—you could be okay someday. Time is the determinant here, and subsequent physical therapy will be vital to your recovery."

He paused here, not wanting to deliver this final prognosis, although it was the last point he would make regarding her condition. He continued, "Unless there is considerable improvement in all of these areas, it's not very likely that you will ever walk again, and it could mean that you could never have children. Having children, frankly, might put your life in jeopardy." Ruby gasped, having heard this news for the first time. Connie closed her eye—it almost snapped shut, sending a sudden gush of tears down her cheek. "Connie, are you with me?"

There was no response. He waited for what seemed forever, but it couldn't have been more than thirty seconds. "Connie?" he repeated, and then he felt her squeeze.

Connie squeezed his hand with a surge of strength. This time, she squeezed twice, and kept on squeezing Dr. von Hoerner's hand. It was her way of screaming no! The possibility that she might not be able to have children was something that had never occurred to her. It was this possibility that upset her the most and the one she felt would be the most difficult to live with.

Dr. von Hoerner had covered what he needed to cover. Clearly, the news was very difficult to take, but he had to deliver it, professionally and personally. He needed to tell Connie these things so that she could begin the healing process. Connie's eye remained closed. He squeezed her hand, let go, and told her that he would leave her now with Ruby and Henry. He looked at them and said, "Stay with her as long as you'd like, of course." After making a notation on the chart to increase the level of Connie's sedatives, he walked out of the room. He figured Connie needed a lot more sleep to get her through the anguish. He'd let the nurse know at the front desk when he walked by, thinking, the sooner the better for Connie.

Ruby and Henry stayed the entire day, even though Connie slept through it, as the sedatives took effect. At six o'clock that evening, they went home. As difficult as it had been to listen to von Hoerner's report, they knew it had been necessary. They would all have to pull together if Connie was ever to return to a life that looked anything like normal.

We human beings wouldn't have gotten this far in our development on this amazing and, sometimes, hostile planet had it not been for an undeniably powerful drive to procreate. The strength of that drive in human beings is the essence of the life force. Those humans who wanted to have children more than anything else are the very ones who have kept our species tumbling forward on the evolutionary trail through every catastrophic event Man and Mother Nature could throw at us. Not every human being has the urge to merge—that unquenchable desire for children—but I can think of one person in particular who did: my mother. But I digress.

CHAPTER THIRTY

The date was August 16, 1947, around noon. It was a Saturday. Ruby and Henry were at home, sitting on the front porch, gazing at Main Street and not at all surprised there wasn't much of the usual Saturday traffic. Connie sat on the porch with them in her wheelchair. She had been home for almost two months. From the time the sun's first rays ran across the roof tops and through the trees, everyone knew the day would be another scorcher, another day of unbearable heat accentuated by high humidity.

That's what these hot, hot, muggy days of August were called in Wisconsin: scorchers—a term that applied whenever the temperature got as high as eighty. There were only a few of them every summer, but they were memorable in their debilitating ability to stop everyone from doing much of anything that required any physical activity. People in Wisconsin just weren't used to that kind of heat. Connie didn't really mind the heat, even though just about every conversation carried with it complaints about it. It felt good to Connie. The heat and humidity seemed to lessen the pain in her hips and legs.

Her recovery was going pretty well, according to most people she spoke with. She had regained some of the weight she had lost at the hospital, thanks mostly to Ruby's cooking, which included a lot of pies, cakes, and cookies. She ate well enough, but her interest in food hadn't returned. The strength in her arms had improved, and she could actually see some muscles returning as a consequence of her daily exercise with a very small pair of weights she had been given by the rehab nurse at St. Agnes at her first return visit to the hospital in late June for a checkup along with some minor cosmetic surgery. She had been going to Appleton more than Fond du Lac lately—almost weekly—to see the oral and eye specialists there. The work on her mouth seemed endless, but the progress was real, and that made her feel better about it.

Her left eye socket had also made some great progress with the placement of a glass eye into what she, to herself, described as the "hole in her head." No one could possibly understand the effect that losing her eye had had on her or how she felt about it, and the impact it had had on her physically, of course. The greatest pain was the pain she was experiencing at the emotional level. What had happened to her eye had a profound impact on her self-image. Connie thought she was hideous, despite all the good work and progress that had been done on her face since she had left the hospital.

Many of the cuts on her face had been superficial. The natural healing powers of her body took care of them, and they had disappeared without leaving any scars. However, there were a couple of big ugly scars that wouldn't go away. One, in particular, ran five inches across her left check, from her upper check bone down to the edge of the left side of her lips. It wasn't pretty, and she didn't think of herself as pretty anymore. And, worse, she thought probably no one else would either. She barely recognized herself in the mirror and cried almost every night, wondering how all of this could have happened to her.

When Connie looked in the mirror, she often recalled that eerie, unsettling moment at the apartment in Appleton on December 15, 1945 when she and Carl were about to leave for the big Christmas party at Schrinsky's, when the reflection in the mirror said, "You will never see me again." Now she understood the comment, but it was totally perplexing. She asked herself again and again, "What was that? Some kind of omen? How could that have happened? How can something like that be?"

Henry, who was seated next to her on the biggest wicker chair on the porch, broke into her thoughts. "Connie," he said, "are you looking forward to the drive up to Rochester tomorrow?"

"Not really, Henry. It's a long drive to Minnesota."

"We'll leave early in the morning but take our time and enjoy the ride, honey. It will be nice to get out of the house and go see some other part of the country."

Henry said this as if Minnesota was adjacent to California and, for him, it was far enough. In his whole life, he had never ever been out of Wisconsin, so this would be an adventure for him. No one should be surprised at the news of his lack of worldliness. In those days, most people, especially in the Midwest, lived their entire lives without leaving the state they were born in, except the soldiers who fought in either World War, of course. Henry was too young to fight in WWI and too old to go overseas in WWII. He was involved in WWII, but his age kept him in Wisconsin doing administrative work for Wisconsin's famed 32nd Infantry Division, a unit of the Army National Guard.

Henry was about one day and two hundred miles from leaving Wisconsin for the first time in his life, although

Rochester was a full 260 miles away, a bit further into Minnesota's heartland. It wasn't the travel that excited him so much. What excited him was the appointment with the specialists at The Mayo Clinic. Henry had heard that the doctors there were the smartest in the world. The clinic's reputation was world renown. Maybe they could do something for Connie to get her back up and about and walking around again, which is what Ruby and Henry hoped for—and so did Connie, despite her low spirits.

Henry continued, "We got a meeting with the doctors there Monday morning. I think at eight in the morning. I'd have to look at the letter I got from them to be sure."

"You think they can really help me, Henry?" asked Connie.

"You betcha, Connie," Henry said, taking a puff on his cigar. "Doc von Hoerner said they were the best in the country. They did everything they could for you at St. Agnes, but the doc said the Mayo Clinic has the specialists, and according to him, they've treated hundreds of patients, some with worse legs than yours." Henry knew that didn't quite sound right, saying 'worse legs than yours,' but he knew Connie understood that he was taking her to the best doctors in the country.

"I hope so, Henry. I hope they can help me," Connie said softly, belying her excitement over the possibilities. "I don't want to think about spending the rest of my life in a wheelchair." That thought really depressed her, and she slipped back into a silent world that was becoming pretty comfortable for her to live in. It was all so awful, and the worst part was the enormous swings in optimism and despair that she'd go through, although she never gave up hope. Connie believed, in the bottom of her heart, despite all of her fears, that she'd walk again; she just didn't know how that would happen. That was the toughest part—not knowing—and she looked to the doctors at The Mayo Clinic to come up with the answers.

A couple of minutes passed in shared silence.

"Criminy," Henry swore, "this scorcher might do me in!" and then drew another puff from his cigar. Connie didn't mind the smoke at all. To her, it meant home, and she always felt safe at home. She never guessed she'd be living at home again, but then again, she never guessed that she'd be in that accident either. In the past couple weeks, a few of her friends had wanted to stop by, but Connie wasn't up to seeing anyone yet. I'd be more honest to say that she didn't want to see them at all. She wasn't ready, she'd tell Ruby. She was unwilling to see the sympathy and maybe shock in their faces when they saw her for the first time since the accident. She just wasn't ready to see anyone or be seen—it was that simple.

A month earlier, a few weeks after Connie had moved in with Ruby and Henry, Carl's parents stopped by the house on Main Street. It was a Sunday, and they offered to take Connie to church at St. Mary's in Chilton. Connie declined because she wasn't ready to go out in public. Besides, it was very difficult meeting with Carl's parents. It was painful for everyone—she could see that—and, on hindsight, it probably wasn't a very good idea, even though it might have seemed so when the invitation was made.

She could see that they had aged a lot since she had last seen them in the early part of December last year. Even though everyone tried to be strong, tears ran throughout their visit, with emotions getting the better of everyone and finally cutting the visit short. A lot of people had a long way to go before they'd get beyond the impact of the accident. Connie wasn't alone on that count.

The heat was oppressively still, like a sauna. There was no movement of air, not even on the open porch. It was stifling. Henry's cigar smoke hung in mid-air, not sure what direction to go. "I'm going to lie down, Henry," Connie said, putting her hands on the wheels of her wheelchair, pivoting it a full one-eighty on the painted wood floor and, with a little burst of energy, making it up the short ramp through the front door and disappearing into the house.

Ruby was out doing the grocery shopping, but Connie didn't need help getting in or out of her wheelchair. She made it easily enough into her bedroom and rolled onto her bed, closed her eyes—although only one eye was real—and tried to remember what her life had been like before the accident. But for whatever reason, those memories didn't come easily. Maybe they were too painful, since they were in such stark contrast to her current life. Her life was so different now. Thankfully, sleep was an escape, taking her into a blissful place, where there were no memories to make her sad. And with it, she became mindless of the heat, thus lessening her discomfort.

Men and women from Wisconsin and Michigan made up the units in the 32nd Infantry Division. During World War I, the 32nd Division was nicknamed "Les Terribles" by the French because of its fortitude in advancing over terrain that other units couldn't get through. Its shoulder patch says it all: it shows a line shot through with a red arrow to signify its tenacity in piercing enemy lines and, ultimately, achieving victory. Whether it's an entire infantry division or one solitary individual, there are countless cases in history where fortitude won the day in conquering what appeared to be the unconquerable. The 32nd Division wasn't the only unit in Wisconsin that would exemplify this kind of fortitude. But I digress.

CHAPTER THIRTY-ONE

On Monday, two days later, Ruby, Henry, and Connie were crossing the Mississippi River with a blood-red sun setting behind them. They were on their way back to Chilton from a long day of diagnosis and follow-up meetings at The Mayo Clinic.

The whole experience had been a huge let down. Ruby, Henry, and Connie had arrived several minutes before eight that morning, in anxious anticipation of a day of testing that would mean—they were so hopeful—that Connie's wheelchair would soon be no longer necessary. By the end of the day, after hours and hours of subjecting Connie to testing, probing, twisting, bending, and turning, not to mention a dozen x-rays, they met in a conference room with several doctors. They were all seated around a large table, where a spokesman, in the presence of the doctors, simply said that the work at St. Agnes had had a maximum impact and there wasn't really anything else they felt they could do.

The doctors at Mayo suspected that Connie had suffered severe bilateral leg peripheral nerve damage, as had been indicated in the medical records they received from St. Agnes, but they couldn't be sure, and they said they couldn't do anything about it. The presenter muttered something about "time will tell." Aside from some miracle or exceptional therapies that they were not yet aware of, the prognosis was bleak. They said Connie should expect to be, for the most part, consigned to a wheelchair the rest of her life, with maybe some limited mobility on crutches. There had simply been too much damage to the nerves in her legs, in their opinion, especially to her left leg, to believe that her legs could function. They said the "skeletal support structure" was insufficient for any sustained walking because of demineralization—in effect, osteoporosis—complicated by severe muscle atrophy. But both of these conditions could be improved with extensive physical therapy; and yet, their recovery might not matter if the nerve damage was permanent.

The doctors said they were sorry and then filed out of the conference room one by one, leaving Ruby, Henry, and Connie alone, stunned with frustration and, worse, hopelessness. Connie had no idea that she could feel so devastated. These men were, after all, specialists and regarded as the best in their field. "How could that be?" and "How could they not be sure?" were questions she asked over and over. At that point, Ruby and Henry stood up, wheeled Connie out of the clinic, and all three got into Henry's car and began the long drive back to Chilton.

Well into the second hour on the road, no one was talking. The silence, like the heat that had settled on the Midwest for the week, was oppressive. The threesome was on the bridge going over the expansive Mississippi River, just above French Island, an island tucked in on the Wisconsin side of the border. The river air carried a slight smell of sewage and decaying vegetation, emanating from the stagnant pools of river water that had collected in the shallows and inlets, where pools had been heating up all day under the hot sun.

The bridge fed into the town of La Crosse, where they

would be spending the night. Henry pulled up to the front of Hotel La Crosse, parked, said he'd be back in a minute, and jumped out of the car. Moments later, he was bounding up a couple of steps and entering the hotel through its ornate double door. He would ask for a suite in the hotel, which he quickly learned meant two adjacent single rooms that had a door between them for easy passage back and forth. Henry would also ask for the first floor to minimize the challenges of getting Connie in and out of the hotel. The desk clerk was very accommodating and handed him a key to each of the two rooms.

Henry returned to the car and shared the news and then began the process of getting Connie into the room. Ruby pulled their suitcases from the backseat, shared by Connie. Henry then lifted Connie's wheelchair out of the trunk, having first untied the straps that secured it in the well of the trunk, and carried it up the front steps to the hotel lobby. It was a fairly routine process for getting Connie from the car to someplace else. In this case, he would carry her up the stairs to the first floor, where she could be placed in her wheelchair and wheeled to the rooms.

Connie hated this experience every time it was repeated. She was, of course, grateful for Henry's strong arms and, when necessary, the care of others, but nothing made her feel as helpless as this public transition, and nothing made her feel that her helplessness was so conspicuous. She didn't want to accept this as a regular occurrence and reminded herself what a disappointment the visit to The Mayo Clinic had been. She had talked to Dr. von Hoerner a while back about improving her mobility, and she'd have to give more thought to his advice, now that help from The Mayo Clinic was no longer a possibility. Connie would have to figure out how to get around on her own, but not now.

The humidity from the river multiplied the discomfort of traveling in the heat, and the temperature seemed to be climbing, although the day was at its end—maybe it had something to do with the river. The three of them had no choice but to stop there. They couldn't make the drive all the way back to Chilton that day, so Henry had elected to check into the only real hotel in this river town. All three travelers were exhausted. Connie couldn't wait to climb into a bed—any bed—and fall asleep. Lately, sleep had become her best escape from a flagging spirit.

It soon became evident that wanting sleep and needing sleep has nothing to do with getting sleep. The midnight hour had passed. Connie lay stretched out on her bed, with just a thin sheet over her. She had quickly dropped her night gown over the side of the bed onto the floor moments after climbing into bed. It was too hot to wear it. The air was still, and the humidity from the river added moisture to it that was at levels unlike anyone in Chilton surely had ever experienced. She was thinking that Mama and Henry must be suffering, like her, in the next room.

The hotel was old, like an elegant old lady, but old nonetheless, and because it was in Wisconsin, cooling systems were rare. There weren't even any ceiling fans, not in the rooms, not even in the lobby or the dining room. Wisconsin building design was dedicated to heating, not cooling. This wasn't the South. Connie's window was open, but air didn't flow in or out. It was as stifling in the room as outside the room. Because of the heat, nobody was moving in town, so traffic noise was essentially nonexistent. Occasionally, she'd hear long and short whistles, which she assumed were made by boats on the river, but she wasn't sure exactly what they came from or what they meant. Their intrusiveness just added to her discomfort.

For an hour, Connie stared at the drab, monochromatic darkness of the ceiling, feeling as if she were an alien on another planet, so remote was her present experience from where she had thought she'd be at this point in her life. The accident had transported her to a different world, and it was a world, at this moment, defined by sweltering heat that was unbearable and air that was unpleasant to breathe. A tear ran out of her eye just then, one of so many that had fallen over the months of surges of despair. She wondered how there could possibly be any more.

The dismal outcome at The Mayo Clinic made her suddenly afraid that she would have to spend the rest of her life in a wheelchair, scarred, and forever bereft of children. "Children?" she whispered to herself, causing more tears to flow. She recalled the prognosis that she probably wouldn't be able to have a baby in her condition. All she had ever truly wanted in life was a child—or two or three! "Now that's unlikely," she thought to herself. She thought some more, and it occurred to her that she might have difficulty getting a husband. And then—it was all too much—as she whispered aloud to herself, "Who'd ever want to marry me?" Connie rolled over onto her stomach, burying her face in the pillow, and started sobbing, feeling entirely lost, spent, and alone in a stuffy room, in an old hotel, in some fetid river town that was as foreign to her as Manchuria and as hot as a summer day in the Congo. Despair moved in on her like a hungry tiger moves in on a tethered lamb. Sleep saved her from being devoured.

THOMAS DUNKER

It is said that adversity teaches us more about ourselves than good fortune, although who would ever prefer the former? No one, of course. But we know that many, many people of good fortune attribute their good fortune to the lessons they learned and the strength they acquired in the face of adversity. But I digress.

CHAPTER THIRTY-TWO

The next day, the silence during their drive across Wisconsin from La Crosse to Chilton continued. It would hang in the car the whole way home, like laundry on a humid day, refusing to let the sunshine make a difference. Connie and Ruby slept a bit en route from time to time, dozing thirty minutes here and there, both having had bouts of sleeplessness the night before, which had deprived them of any sense that it was a new day and good news was still out there, somewhere. Surely it was somewhere: they just didn't know where.

Henry drove with stoicism, his focus on the road and a lit cigar in his hand—the hand resting on the top of the steering wheel. Every once in a while a heady ash that had cooled blew off the hot end of his cigar and swirled in a whirlwind of air caused by the open windows before flying out one of them into the lush farmlands of central Wisconsin. The swirl of ashes didn't bother anyone; it meant that the car was moving, and that provided some relief from the heat. It helped, too, that they were moving away from the Mississippi River and onto higher ground.

The drive would take them all day, going through small towns and farm hamlets, which seemed to be perfectly spaced at twenty-minute intervals. Many of those "towns" were just intersections, and some didn't even appear on a map. Up ahead was Wisconsin Dells, which was a real town, one with a downtown shopping district. The next two towns of any real interest were Waupun, where the state prison had been located since 1851 and then, the largest town in their path, Fond du Lac. They would drive through Fond du Lac without stopping, as they had done two days earlier. But now, with nearly a hundred miles already behind them, they were ready to take a break.

They stopped for lunch in Wisconsin Dells, which was famous for its interesting and unusual geology, specifically, glacial carving of the rocky, river terrain. This was so uncommon and beautiful that the town had become quite the tourist destination. Henry ordered some sandwiches to go from one of the restaurants on Broadway, the main drag, while Ruby and Connie waited in the car. They would then seek a park or a lookout and eat in the car. It was too difficult for Connie to go into restaurants because the buildings didn't have any wheelchair access.

Getting around in a wheelchair was virtually impossible and a painful and inescapable reminder of Connie's predicament. But this also provided the impetus to do something to get out of that wheelchair. She had one very bad leg and one that was still pretty good, although it also needed some serious rehab. Maybe she could still do something about this on her own, now that there weren't any other options. Connie sensed that from here on, it was all up to her. That's all she thought about the rest of the way home.

The threesome pulled up to the front of the house on Main Street in the late afternoon. It was good to be home. Now they had some answers, and everyone could give some thought to what Connie would do next.

Here's an interesting quote from W.H. Murray of the

Scottish Himalayan Expedition:

> *"Until one is committed, there is hesitancy, the chance to draw back, always ineffectiveness. Concerning all acts of initiative (and creation) there is one elementary truth, the ignorance of which kills countless ideas and splendid plans: that the moment one definitely commits oneself, then, Providence moves too. All sorts of things occur to help one that would never otherwise have occurred. A whole stream of events issues from the decision, raising in one's favor all manner of unforeseen incidents and meetings and material assistance, which no man could have dreamed would have come his way. I have learned a deep respect for one of Goethe's couplets: 'Whatever you can do, or dream you can, begin it. Boldness has genius, power and magic in it.'"*

But I digress.

CHAPTER THIRTY-THREE

On August 20th, two days after the trip to The Mayo Clinic, Connie committed to what she called her Personal Recovery Plan, and it started with two resolutions: 1) she would be upbeat, positive, and cheery in all matters from then on, and 2) she would walk again, despite the ugly odds that had been given to her. The Plan, as she called it, was formulated during her sleeplessness that night, and when she arose in the morning, she was ready to begin what she thought of as her new life.

It had been an easy decision to make. She had come to it because every other alternative was unpleasant for her and, surely, would be unpleasant for anyone in contact with her. She didn't delude herself that it would be easy to implement; it would take a commitment that would require conscientious effort at all times. The first part of The Plan, the part about "think happy thoughts"—the phrase that best described her new-found course of action—was something that could begin right away. The second part of The Plan was the big unknown. Given what she knew about her present situation, she didn't expect any miracles and surely assumed she would be in a wheelchair for quite some time, but, she would say to others, "Not forever!"

The implementation of her Plan didn't mean that her behavior that morning was so dramatically different that

154

everyone noticed, but months later, people were describing her as upbeat, outgoing, and a joy to be with, even though she was still in a wheelchair.

Another big event in Connie's life happened later that same day when Connie was in the kitchen with Ruby peeling apples for one of her mama's homemade apple pies. Henry walked into the house and headed to the kitchen, calling out in his booming voice, "Hellooooooo, I'm home."

Ruby and Connie returned his greeting as he walked into the kitchen and gave Ruby a big kiss on the cheek and then took a step to the kitchen table and leaned over and gave Connie a kiss on the forehead.

"We're making apple pie for dinner, Henry." Connie stated with glee. "We know you love apple pie!"

"You betcha, Connie," Henry said, "nothin' better than your mama's apple pie!"

Connie picked up on a little extra energy from Henry. "So," she inquired, "why the big smile?"

Henry turned to Ruby, and then Ruby asked him, "So you got it?" He was nodding to her and smiling, and then he looked at Connie.

"Got what?" asked Connie?

"Go see for yourself," Henry replied. "Go look in the box in the front yard."

"What is it? Is it something for me?"

"It's for you, all right, but you gotta look to find out."

Connie backed up from the table, pivoted her chair, and wheeled past Ruby and Henry, out the kitchen, through the dining room, through the living room, through the front door, and rolled down the ramp at wheelchair-expert speed into the yard. Ruby and Henry were right behind her. Connie rolled up to a big cardboard box at the end of the walkway that was open at the top. She leaned over, her neck extended over the opening, and right away she saw a puppy, a little black cocker spaniel! It whimpered upon seeing her, and when she put her hand down to it, she got a lot of licks.

"Oh Mama! Oh Henry! He's so cute!" She put one hand under his soft belly and scooped him up right into her lap. "He's soooooooooooooooo cute!" Connie then raised the little pup in both hands just above her head and went nose to nose with him. "Hello you little puppy. You're soooo adorable, aren't you? Yes you are... you are so cute!" Connie let the pup lick her face, and then she looked at Ruby and Henry. "Is he... oops," she checked the underside of the puppy before continuing, "Is she... is she ours? Please say yes! Is she?"

Ruby deferred to Henry. "No, Connie, she's not ours." And he paused for one second, for effect, and said, "She's yours!"

Connie let out a little yelp of happiness. "Oh, thank you, thank you, thank you," she repeated over and over, nuzzling the puppy, which she had already decided was perfect. "She's the cutest... just the cutest little thing I think I have ever seen—ever."

"So we should keep her?" asked Ruby.

"Yes, Mama! Of course!" And the three of them laughed—such a happy scene it was.

"What's her name?" Connie asked.

"That's up to you," Henry replied.

Connie lifted the pup in both hands again, holding her over her head once more, almost nose to nose, and looked her right in her little deep brown eyes and paused only for a second before saying, "Your name is Penny! Yes, Penny it will be because you are my lucky Penny!" And then Connie brought

Penny down to her chest and tucked the little black ball of fur under her chin. The afternoon sun shone on both of them, and Connie felt a lightheartedness and happiness that she hadn't felt in a long time.

How we love our dogs! They are truly man's best friend. We enjoy a symbiotic friendship with them that goes back thousands of years. At the end of the ice age, Man tamed wolves and, through careful selection and interbreeding, created the multitude of dog breeds we know today. This means that dogs have been domesticated for a very long time. They have grown and evolved with us in domestic harmony.

The famous chimpanzee anthropologist Jane Goodall said that our relationship with dogs, unlike with chimpanzee (the species closest to us genetically) "is not related to intelligence, but the desire to help, to be obedient, to gain approval." This unique relationship has contributed over the millennia to a mutually successful strategy for survival, and as we know, dogs have helped us through some pretty tough moments. But I digress.

CHAPTER THIRTY-FOUR

It was the last week of September. Another Indian Summer was in play in central Wisconsin. Connie sat in her wheelchair in the front yard on Main Street, enjoying the warmth of the midday sunshine. She had just wheeled herself up the street for several blocks and back again with Penny scampering at her side the whole way. It was a good workout, and when she returned to her yard, she rested. She liked the openness of sitting in the sun or in the dappled shade under the giant elms that sat on the corners of the property. Fresh air, to her, was the perfect tonic for the small rooms in the house and the limitations of her wheelchair. Even on rainy days, she wanted to sit outside, but Ruby insisted that she stay under the shelter of the front porch.

Today was a glorious day, a day with sunshine, a faint breeze, and very little humidity. The leaves on the trees had lost their luster and now hung on aging stems in the prelude to autumn. They rippled when a soft breeze ran through them, but not enough to suggest to anyone that it was a windy day. Penny jumped up into Connie's lap and snuggled into the blanket that Connie had thrown over her legs. Connie then looked upward, into the sun's warmth, closed her eyelids, and recalled the first days with Penny. Her memory of the first day that she and Penny had played fetch made her smile.

Penny could play fetch all day if someone would play with

her. Henry was the first to discover Penny's love for fetching when he threw her toys into the front yard one Saturday from the porch. Once Henry had discovered Penny's talent for fetching, he got his hands on a rubber ball and tossed it into the yard. Penny was all over it in a heartbeat, and brought it back to him every time. He was having fun with the game and pleasantly surprised at Penny's retrieving instincts. After making Penny do a few runs into every corner of the front yard, he chucked the ball into the apple orchard in the lot next to the house. It landed beyond the first row of apple trees into some very tall grass. Penny followed the flight path of the ball and went after it like a rocket before it was lost from Henry's sight. But in less than a minute, the ball was at Henry's feet. She was an all-star.

Connie basked in the warmth of the sun's rays and enjoyed recalling the events of that day when Penny's obsession for fetching had become evident. Connie was confident that anybody could throw anything and, as long as Penny saw it, she'd get it and bring it back to the thrower's feet.

Unfortunately, the fact that Connie was in a wheelchair presented something of a challenge for Connie and Penny to work out. Because Connie's feet weren't on the ground, Penny didn't really figure them into the equation. Instead, the wheels of the wheelchair seemed to be feet to Penny, so she would drop the ball at the base of either wheel. The very first time this happened, they both realized the problem. Without uncomfortable contortions, Connie wasn't able to reach the ball at the base of either wheel. Her fingertips were about two inches too short, but it was a long two inches for her to overcome from the wheelchair.

This obstacle to playing fetch led to a profound

demonstration of Penny's intelligence. Penny solved the problem. The solution was so astounding that Mama and Henry had trouble believing Connie when she told them about it. To prove it, Connie set it up later that day so that Penny would have to repeat her trick. The demonstration began with her request of Henry to clear the area around her wheelchair, specifically, to get rid of the apples on the ground. Penny had to be restrained while Henry threw them back into the orchard. Apparently, Henry thought to himself, cleaning up the apples was necessary for the performance of the trick. Connie was ready and confident that Penny would repeat her trick.

Connie then got Penny's attention and threw the ball across the yard, toward the orchard. Penny returned it to her to no one's surprise, dropping the ball at the base of the wheel of Connie's wheelchair. As Ruby and Henry watched, Penny and Connie stared at each other, just as they had earlier over the same impasse. The ball sat on the ground, just out of Connie's reach, inches below her fingertips.

"Go, Penny, help me," Connie said, pointing to the orchard, "Get some apples!"

Suddenly, Penny spun and ran away, heading for the orchard. Seconds later, she returned with an apple in her mouth and dropped it next to the ball, where Connie simply sat, waited, and watched. Penny turned around and ran to the orchard again, returning in seconds with another apple, which she dropped alongside the first one. Both Ruby and Henry watched this process unfolding, neither able to guess what would happen. Penny made a few more trips, and then Connie counted six apples on the ground, fairly bunched together near her wheel, all just below her fingertips, but none in a better position than the rubber ball.

Penny stopped at the base of the wheel, overseeing all six apples and the ball, and looked up at Connie. After a few moments of panting, Penny picked up the rubber ball and gently placed it on top of the apples. To everyone's surprise, but apparently not to Penny's, the ball was now within the grasp of Connie's fingertips. Game on!

Connie praised Penny and beamed over Penny's intelligence. Ruby and Henry applauded, quite in disbelief over what they had just witnessed, but they couldn't deny it because they'd just seen it.

After that amazing apple trick encore, Henry left an overturned wooden fruit box at the corner of the walkway and sidewalk so that Penny would have a readymade platform for the ball after each retrieval.

It was a good memory for Connie, and it pushed a couple of the bad ones aside.

From then on, whenever Connie and Penny played fetch, Penny literally danced in circles around Connie's wheelchair, when her nose wasn't fixed on the rubber ball that sat on the overturned box. Two hours of fetch with Penny every day was just fine with Connie, an hour in the morning and one after lunch. During each hour, she spent roughly thirty minutes throwing the ball with each arm as far as she could. Even in one month of fetch with Penny, Connie could feel the difference in her arms and noted that every few days she was able to throw the ball farther than before. Nothing made Penny happier—and Connie, too, enjoyed their game, especially whenever she threw the ball farther than ever. It was a good sign that she was getting stronger.

The weeks passed, and warm days had given in to cooler ones; autumn was well underway. Cold nights had already made their presence known, as windows were no longer left open at night, not even a crack. Air that was already too cold trumped fresh air, so the windows would stay closed until spring arrived.

Every day Connie would work on her legs and arms. The arms were easy to exercise. She had her two-pound barbells and, when the weather permitted, a game of fetch. Exercising the legs wasn't as easy, but she had figured out a way to do some work on them. For this part of her Plan, with the help of a couple of elastic, wraparound bandages, she would fix each hand weight to an ankle and then lift her legs at the hip, making her knees rise upward so that her feet would rise off the footrest of the wheelchair.

In mid-August when she first tried this leg-lifting exercise, neither foot moved, not even once in the entire first week. Not only were the leg muscles seemingly non-existent in each leg at that time, but the feeling in her bad leg, the left one, hadn't returned. That leg was almost entirely numb, as it had been since she had left the hospital.

There was no doubt that this absence of feeling was attributable to nerve damage, and it presented the question that no one could answer, not at St. Agnes, not at The Mayo Clinic, not anywhere: Was the nerve damage permanent or was the nerve simply caught in a slow healing process? Dr. von Hoerner reminded her that nerves are, indeed, very slow to regenerate and that she shouldn't lose hope. Connie refused to accept the possibility that the nerve damage was permanent.

She tied the weights to her feet every day in the ensuing weeks and continued with her daily commitment to think only happy thoughts. Thus, she remained upbeat and optimistic, despite the pain and frustration. Progress in lifting her legs was miniscule, but by the end of September, she could lift her knees a couple of inches, and then in October, a couple of more inches. It was progress, slow and steady, but progress nonetheless.

Connie and Penny had developed a bond that made them inseparable. There was no doubt that Penny was, indeed, Connie's dog. Not surprisingly, Penny followed Connie everywhere; she went where Connie went. She spent hours on Connie's lap when Connie was reading and, to no one's surprise, slept on Connie's bed every night.

This story about my mother is based on the truth, although, perhaps not surprisingly, a few blanks have had to be filled in where the truth wasn't known. An eye witness to Penny's cleverness told me that story about Penny and a few others and added that he had enjoyed telling that particular story many times over the years because he never forgot that remarkable display of intelligence by Penny the dog. Did I already say we love our dogs? You bet I did. But I digress.

CHAPTER THIRTY-FIVE

Connie's dedication to her rehabilitation continued through the winter. It was exhausting work—frustrating too—and it brought her to the brink of despair on many occasions. Her life was mostly about recovery, and her days were extremely repetitive. She exercised and exercised, following a rigorous routine where little or no progress was visible for achingly long periods of time. As many as three weeks would pass before she could register a milestone in the number of times she had lifted a weight or the amount of weight she had lifted. But progress was made, inch by painful inch, minute by painful minute.

By the middle of March, 1948, her right leg had strengthened sufficiently that she could rise from her wheelchair and stand on it. In a standing position, she would bend the knee slightly, only for a moment or two, before standing tall again and testing its ability to support her weight. "Such a simple process, and it still hurts a lot," she thought to herself. But despite considerable pain, she remained committed to The Plan. The right leg was definitely getting better. Would she ever be able to walk on it? She didn't know, but she did know that the previous November she hadn't even been able to stand on it.

Progress on her left leg was a lot slower. The feeling had come back to some extent. The extensive numbness that she had lived with for so long had dissipated, but some areas were still numb, and she wasn't close to being able to put all of her weight on it. Both legs, it seemed to her, hurt with the damp and cold weather. She assumed that all the steel pins in her pelvis and leg bones accounted for much of that discomfort. She thought that if only she knew how to interpret each bit of stiffness that came and went with the changes in the weather, she could forecast rain and snow and sleet. As it was, although she didn't think she was clairvoyant, she could see a future of incessant aches and pains in her bones. Lately, she sensed more aches in her left leg than her right and wondered if that meant that the nerves in the left leg were repairing themselves. She thought about that for a while and concluded, "If that's the case, then bring it on!"

In the first days of April, her old friend Virginia Stranski popped in to say hi. In February, 1946, a month before Connie and Carl had gotten married, Virginia had married and moved to—where else?—Virginia! where her husband had some kind of secret job with the Navy out of Norfolk Navy Base. She was in Chilton for two days visiting her parents and was so excited to see Connie again. It was the first time they had seen each other since Connie's wedding to Carl.

Connie was slowly getting over her altered appearance, although this was probably the biggest adjustment in her quest to return to some kind of life she could feel good about. The person she saw in the mirror was a stranger to the memories of herself. Even so, she was thankful for the progress she had made with the cosmetic surgery to her face, although some pretty serious red lines still zigged across her cheeks. The area around her left eye was healing, although she didn't think for a second that anyone would mistake her glass eye for a real one. It caused considerable discomfort and would, she was told, require more surgery in the orbital area in the years to come. It was one more change that she had to accept, along with so many others. Fixating on any one of her maladies was something she carefully avoided, but not easily.

Connie's weight had climbed back closer to normal, although she was still very thin. It was a big improvement over being emaciated, which was how she had looked the previous summer. Connie had made a lot of progress, and except for the wheelchair and the pain in her legs, she was pleased with her Personal Recovery Plan. If you asked her outright if it was working, she'd say yes! not that anyone knew she had a specific program in place, especially something she called her Personal Recovery Plan.

Virginia stepped up to the porch on Main Street at about two o'clock that day. She stamped her feet free of some snow that was slow to melt with the encroaching spring, and then stepped right up to the front door and rang the bell. She remembered the sound of the simple four-note chime from having heard it hundreds of times in the past. The memory of it made her smile. She was so excited about seeing Connie and had heard enough about what Connie had gone through that she was sure she wouldn't be shocked when she saw her. They had only spoken on the phone a couple of times over the last few years. Distance had taken its toll on the regular and frequent calls they had shared years ago. Both regretted that they had lost touch, but friendships like theirs were not easily displaced by time or distance.

Ruby opened the door with a big smile on her face and greeted Virginia warmly. Behind Ruby, Virginia caught a glimpse of Connie in the wheelchair. Virginia paused long enough for a quick hug and a hello to Ruby and then went right to Connie. Ruby understood. The two girls, after all, had been best friends growing up and then rooming together at the University of Wisconsin in Madison.

Virginia was shocked at Connie's appearance and, for a fleeting moment, not even sure it was Connie in the wheelchair, so altered was Connie's appearance from Virginia's memories of the youthful and beautiful golden girl she had known all her life. Tears flooded Virginia's eyes. She would have to pass them off as tears of joy over their reunion, but the crocodile-sized tears that ran down her face were all about sympathy. Virginia's heart twisted and her stomach tightened up with such a wave of sorrow that, had she not hugged Connie immediately, she might have fallen to the floor on her knees. She closed her eyes and let the joy of their reunion overcome her sympathy for Connie, and she was suddenly overwhelmed with the happiness of being together again with her oldest and dearest friend.

They had missed each other terribly and found it difficult to pull themselves apart. Penny joined in the exchange of the deep emotions of the moment, circling the wheelchair with two-legged hops and leaps, while simultaneously trying to get into Connie's lap and getting a few good licks onto Virginia's tearful face.

"Penny! Down!" Connie commanded, to absolutely no effect.

"Oh God, Connie," Virginia was the first to speak, "I have missed you so much, and I don't know how you made it through everything you went through... but you look wonderful to me!" And Virginia hugged Connie ferociously again, still bent over her, but now with a dog wedged in between the two of them.

"Oh Virginia," Connie stammered, so overwhelmed at seeing her old friend again and not realizing how much she had missed her. "Oh, Virginia," Connie repeated, swallowing through her own strong emotions, "You look wonderful, and I have missed you so much!" Their emotions almost overwhelmed them. They would have to find more comfortable positions if they were to say anything else to each other.

Ruby broke in, "Connie, you and Virginia should move into the living room. Let her make herself comfortable, and you two catch up there. Virginia, would you like some coffee or tea?" Ruby asked graciously.

"Tea would be great, Ruby, thank you." She couldn't take her eyes off of Connie. "One sugar, no cream, please."

"And you, Connie?" Ruby asked, "the usual?"

"Yes, Mama, thank you, maybe an extra sugar this time." Ruby disappeared into the kitchen.

Virginia flopped onto the old worn silk sofa in the living room following Ruby's gesture to make herself comfortable. Connie rolled into the room right behind her and then parked her wheelchair so that she was face to face with Virginia when Virginia sat down. They both leaned forward and held onto each other's hands and, for the next hour, caught up over tea in a flurry of conversation.

It was a happy conversation, just as Connie had hoped for. Connie had been careful not to say anything that would trigger sympathy or sadness, although it had been clear to her that Virginia was shocked by her appearance. But what was one to do with that observation other than keep moving forward and getting on with life? She was determined to be upbeat, and the energy registered with her old friend as their conversation began to flow into laughter and giggles loud enough that Ruby could hear a new-found merriment coming out of the living room.

About an hour later, in the midst of their joyous reunion, Virginia shared her biggest news.

"Connie. I didn't tell you that John and I had been trying so hard since we got married to have a baby." Connie went still with the introduction of this topic and actually held her breath to hear where Virginia's opening was going. "Well," Virginia continued, "we started to think I'd never get pregnant." Virginia paused, and Connie's eyebrows went up as if to say, "and?" Virginia leaned forward, whispering, as if a conspiracy were in the making, "We did it a lot, you know, every day, sometimes a couple of times a day." She was blushing now.

Connie burst out, "You're pregnant!"

"Yes!" Virginia almost squealed with delight, "I'm pregnant! Finally! I'm pregnant!" Virginia repeated jubilantly. The two friends reached out to each other and held hands again over the exciting news.

"Mama," Connie called out, directing her voice to the kitchen, "Virginia's pregnant! Mama, did you hear that? Virginia's pregnant!"

Ruby appeared from around the corner just then with a tea pot of freshly brewed tea, the steam rising from the spout. "My oh my, Virginia! Isn't that wonderful?" Ruby exclaimed, "How exciting!"

"When's the baby due?" Connie interjected. "You're not even showing!"

"It's barely the third month, so in October, we think the 28th," replied Virginia. All three women looked at each other and smiled. This was wonderful news, and it was evident from their expressions.

"Oh Virginia," Connie said, "I'm so happy for you and John." And she was happy of course, but she also felt a huge pang of sadness with her recollection of Dr. von Hoerner's words to her many months ago that made it clear she probably couldn't have a child of her own and, if she did, it might be very risky, maybe even life-threatening.

The two old friends visited for another half an hour before Virginia left. They wouldn't see each other again during Virginia's visit to Chilton that week, but they parted with a renewed commitment to do a better job of staying in touch.

When Ruby and Connie heard Virginia's car drive away, Ruby looked at Connie and saw the sadness in Connie's eyes and knew exactly what was behind it.

"Connie," Ruby said, "as wonderful as Virginia's news is, I know it was difficult to hear, honey. We can be happy for her and thankful for her good fortune. You have a wonderful friend in Virginia, and you two will always be friends and share in each other's joys and sorrows. We can never be sure what the future has in store for us, Connie. And while I've always told you that life isn't a bowl of cherries, that doesn't mean there won't be some wonderful surprises ahead."

"I know, Mama," Connie responded a bit sullenly, "I know."

Ruby continued, "You're going through a very difficult and trying time in your life, and you will get through this. Someday, you'll look back and your life will be better and all of this will be nothing but a distant memory."

Ruby leaned over at this point and clasped Connie's head between her loving hands and kissed her on both cheeks. "You know Henry and I love you very much, and so many other people do too. We're all rooting for you." Connie nodded but said nothing. "You'll make it through all this, honey, and you'll have a good life. Mark my words."

Ruby gathered up the empty tea cups and moved toward the kitchen, calling out to Connie, "Now why don't you bundle up, take Penny out to the porch with you for some fresh air, and watch the sun melt the snow away before it gets dark." As she entered the kitchen, she added, "I bet Penny wouldn't mind fetching that old ball a little bit either!" Penny raced to the front door, perfectly aware that some good ol' fetching was about to begin. "Fetch" was a word she knew, and it was one of her favorites, right up there with "cookie"!

There's nothing like a reunion between old friends. Anyone who's been reunited with an old friend after having been separated for a long time knows how easy it is to pick up the relationship right where it left off, as if hardly a day had passed. That's an amazing thing about friendships, and it's a wonderful feeling that we can pick up where we left off. Of course, that's just a feeling. The truth is that we don't really pick up where we left off—not exactly—because life keeps moving forward and affects us in both expected and unexpected ways. We can never pick up exactly where we left off, but it's a mighty good feeling to know that we can carry so much forward with us to make it seem that way.

Meeting up with old friends is especially nice because the memories we carry forward are, more likely than not, of the good things that were shared. And that's what we should carry forward—the good things. All the rest is best kept in the past, where, if we're lucky, it can fade away. It's your call, of course. I know what I prefer. I say let the good memories prevail! But I digress.

CHAPTER THIRTY-SIX

Penny wouldn't stop barking. Her excitement was too much for her compact cocker spaniel frame to contain. She jumped onto Connie's bed and then down to the floor, repeating the frenzy of leaping over and over again from bed to floor and from floor to bed, pausing long enough at each u-turn to spin in a circle like a dervish-crazed dog each time she landed on a different surface. The two bedroom windows in this corner room were wide open, inviting the fresh June air into the room. It occurred to Connie that Penny might actually jump through one of them, so crazed was she in her behavior.

Penny was barking at Connie the whole time. It was the first time that Connie had stood up on her own—two feet away from the wheelchair—and tried to walk. Connie's presence in this fully vertical posture was something new to Penny and so strange that it rousted the poor dog into a reaction that Connie hadn't anticipated. Penny's barking continued unabated as Connie took slow and careful steps from the bed to her bureau, which was six feet away. One minute and twelve very small steps later, Connie stood at her dressing bureau, her palms planted squarely on its surface, and looked into the mirror at the triumphant expression on her face.

"I did it," she declared to herself, "I can walk!"

Penny wouldn't stop barking, which is what drew Ruby to Connie's bedroom. Ruby burst into the room, not knowing what to expect, fearful that something awful had happened to Connie. "Connie!" Ruby cried out when she saw her daughter standing in front of the bureau. She froze in surprise, not sure that she could believe her eyes.

Connie turned to her. "Mama! I can walk! Look, I can walk!" she cried out as tears of joy appeared in her eyes. She had done what the doctors had said she'd probably never do. They had prepared her for the worst, but she'd never lost sight of her goal.

Ruby and Connie went to each other in two steps and hugged in an embrace of such strong emotions that, for a second, it was difficult for either one of them to breathe. They both sobbed with unbounded happiness in a mutual love that mothers feel for their daughters and daughters feel for their mothers, a profound belief in the power of a kind of nurturing love that maternalism gives wings too, all this while Penny stood on her hind legs, determined to get between the two of them! It was undeniably and indescribably an exciting moment for all three of them!

Connie's separation from her wheelchair happened almost immediately. A day later, it was designated obsolete and removed from the house, vanquished by Henry to St. Agnes's inventory in exchange for some crutches. Full feeling had returned to both of her legs, and a year of soulful commitment, determination in the face of pain, and therapeutic exercise had given her the muscle and bone strength to take those first steps. There was still a ways to go, and walking didn't come easily because fatigue would set in quickly, but over the following weeks, with the help of crutches, the fatigue gradually lessened. Connie's bone and muscle mass had returned, and by the end of summer, the need for crutches was greatly diminished.

On September 4th, 1948, the crutches were no longer necessary and they were relegated to a corner under the basement steps of the house on Main Street in Chilton, Wisconsin.

For the next four months, Connie's rehabilitation continued along with numerous cosmetic and dental surgeries. Of course, her physical therapy continued with weights, but the long walks through the quiet little town of Chilton were what helped her the most. Her right leg had fully recovered, but her left leg still hurt with a pain that was so deep that she couldn't exactly locate its source. It didn't take much of a walk to remind her that her recovery in that leg was not and probably would never be one hundred percent.

She also had a lot of healing to do emotionally. In many ways, that healing was the slowest, as those wounds were perhaps the deepest and might never completely heal. She thought of Carl often, mostly when she was in bed late at night, while she laid awake several hours after Ruby and Henry had fallen asleep. She'd stare at the blackness of the ceiling, remembering a lifetime that no longer seemed to have been hers, with Penny snoring in the middle of the bed, often butted sideways against her hips. Penny snored, and in a funny way, it reminded Connie of Carl. He didn't snore really, but Penny's heavy breathing and sudden snorts sometimes woke Connie up out of her dreams, and for a millionth of a second, she thought it was Carl's breathing that she had heard. With time, fewer tears in the darkness would run down her face, until at some point, they would cease, and sleep would once again take over. Time heals all.

Not only does life go on, as we all well know, whether we

are participating in it or not, but as we get older, it also goes by a lot faster. The frequency that we say "Time flies!" to friends escalates fiendishly fast, especially when we are having fun. When we aren't having fun or are simply faced with the monotony of dealing with the necessities of life, we look at the clock and wish time would go faster. What a mistake that is! Time goes by fast enough on its own, whatever is or is not happening. But I digress.

CHAPTER THIRTY-SEVEN

In February, 1949, Gimbels was the largest chain of department stores in the country, one that had grown from a carefully cultivated rivalry with Macy's, and its popularity rose the previous winter with all the publicity that came with the release of the movie "Miracle on 34th Street." It was the biggest and best department store in Milwaukee. It's where Connie worked on the second floor in sales in the women's clothing section. It was the first week in February and the first week of her first job since the accident.

Gimbels was on Wisconsin Avenue, Milwaukee's main downtown street, in an eight-story building that loomed over the Milwaukee River, its front door within a few feet of a drawbridge that went up and down all day long in the summer, but rarely in the winter. The Milwaukee River was covered by an ice floe, as it usually was every February. River traffic this time of year was nearly non-existent, so the drawbridge didn't get much of a workout. This was a good thing, as its closure meant that the steady streams of shoppers and business people could move up and down the avenue without having to stand still in freezing weather waiting for the bridge to go down. And this flow of people meant a steady flow of people going in and out of the store.

On her fourth day of work, it was snowing hard—big Nutcracker Ballet snowflakes, which collected on hats and shoulders, snowflakes that had crystalline patterns that were so big that it was easy to see that no two were alike. People brought them into the store with them, alight on their winter hats and coats, if they didn't get brushed off first. The biggest snowflakes made it up the single file escalator to the second floor before succumbing to a meltdown.

Lots of snowflakes made it up there on the shoulders of one woman's gorgeous floor-length mink coat. She was a rather plain woman, almost diminutive, in her late thirties. She moved slowly in her dark fur coat with matching hat, looking like what an iceberg might look like in the night: massive, dark, unstoppable, but indeed she stopped, right in front of Connie who, standing over the counter of couture gloves, was mesmerized by the woman's approach. Connie had never seen so much fur on one creature, unless it was the grizzly bear that was mounted on its hind feet, claws extended, at the Milwaukee Museum of Natural History, poised to attack. This customer, however, was not poised to attack. And, in fact, Connie's second impression, the one subsequent to the grizzly bear image, was one of a woman who was definitely not feeling well and, possibly, in need of assistance.

Connie quickly stepped around the counter, ignoring the tweak of pain in her left leg, as if to personally welcome the woman into the department, but her intentions were much more altruistic.

"Hello," Connie said in her friendliest tone, as she approached within a few feet of the fur-bundled woman, "Forgive me, but would you like to sit down and rest for a minute and catch your breath?"

The woman smiled uneasily back, clearly fatigued. "Yes," she replied, seemingly in some discomfort, "Yes, that would be nice. Thank you."

Connie instinctively took the woman by an arm and led her past a couple of clothing racks toward a wall of the store that was near some mirrors and the changing rooms, where she knew there were a couple of chairs. The massive amount of fur that Connie's arm was suddenly wrapped around wasn't lost on her. The coat was very distinctive. Besides being a full-length mink coat, it had large lapels that, when turned up, fully collared the wearer's head in fur, and the sleeves ended in cuffs that were so deep they could have been made into stoles with no loss to the coat's good standing as a coat. Connie had never seen cuffs that big. "Maybe," Connie thought to herself, "it was the weight of the coat that was causing her fatigue."

"May I help you with your coat?" Connie offered, "You might feel more comfortable with it off. It's warm in here."

The customer assented in silence, turning her back to Connie and allowing her to help her with the very heavy coat. Connie set it on one of the chairs along with the fur hat that had been handed to her as well. When she looked at the woman, she was shocked to see how thin she was. The coat had masked her frailty.

"Here," Connie said, with the chair in front of them at last, "sit here a minute. Rest a bit. May I get you a glass of water?" she offered.

The now furless woman nodded and with some difficulty said, "Thank you, yes. Water would be nice."

Connie went into the dressing room area and through a service door where she knew she could get some water for the customer and returned within a minute, a full glass in hand. The customer appeared to have caught her breath but looked no better for it.

"Here's some water for you. Maybe this will help." Connie put the glass into the woman's outstretched hand and noticed a very slight tremor in it as she grasped the glass on her own and raised it to her mouth for a sip before lowering it.

"Thank you. Thank you for your kindness," the woman in fur said and continued, "I haven't been feeling well lately... been undergoing treatments for cancer."

This bit of news was certainly not good. "Oh," Connie said, a bit surprised over the woman's candor, "I'm so sorry."

The customer drank again from the glass of water and looked up at Connie. "You've been so kind. What's your name?"

"My name is Connie."

"Really?" replied the customer. "It's a pleasure to meet you, Connie. My name is Connie, too." She put her right hand out to offer a handshake.

Connie shook the customer's hand and said, "It's nice to meet you too, Connie,"

The frail woman then asked, "Is your name from Constance or Consuelo?"

"Constance."

"Mine too," the woman replied and softly smiled, adding no other comment.

Connie then said, "Please rest here as long as you need to, but I have to get back to my counter."

"Oh, certainly, and... and thank you again Connie. I hope I can return the favor someday."

With that, Connie returned to the counter, with the slightest limp, and took up her sales position once again, looking for ways she could assist other customers.

A half hour later, Connie returned to the chairs by the

dressing room. The fur-coated woman had departed, and an empty glass was on the floor under the chair that she had been seated on.

At the end of the day, on the bus on her way back to the Catholic Women's Residence, where she had leased a room on a monthly basis, Connie thought about the woman she had helped and how she'd never seen so much mink on one person and how deathly pale its owner had looked. She also noticed her left leg throbbing softly but steadily with pain and wondered if she would be able to stand at a counter day after day. She decided she would try to stick it out for a few more weeks, maybe even a month or two—maybe it was just something one gets used to, and after a while, she'd be fine on her feet all day. If the pain didn't subside after a while, she'd have to find a different kind of job. She would call Mama and Henry that night, since they'd asked her to call them every night to let them know how her new life in Milwaukee was going.

Anyone who has ever stood on their feet for an entire workday will readily understand the physical challenge presented by that. I had a job once in the summer between my freshman and sophomore years of college working in a foundry in Milwaukee. My job was to stand at a spinning metal brush all day and knock the rust off of hundreds of eight-inch bolts, one at a time, that were piled in a big bin parked next to me. I don't know what was more difficult, gripping rusty bolts in my hands all day long with the pressure of a metal brush ripping at them or standing on my feet all day in front of the spinning metal brush. I quit at the end of the first week and went back to giving tennis lessons. I don't really remember the pain in my arms, but I haven't forgotten how sore my legs were at the end of each day. Standing all day is tough work. But I digress.

CHAPTER THIRTY-EIGHT

George Dunker's office was on the opposite side of the street from Gimbels and on the other side of the bridge, a few blocks east, toward Lake Michigan. It was on the fourteenth floor of a very large office building that covered nearly one square block in the heart of Milwaukee's downtown commercial area. The massive building housed hundreds of businesses in its offices, such as law firms, manufacturing rep offices, and a lot of doctors' offices. George Dunker was a medical doctor, specifically, an otorhinolaryngologist, which was a long name for a specialist in disorders of the eye, ear, nose, and throat.

Dr. Dunker stood at one of the windows in his private office within a suite of five rooms. His office was on a south wall that looked out onto Wisconsin Avenue, over a hundred feet below. It was a gray day, late in the afternoon, a wintry day in the middle of an April in which winter just wouldn't let go. The sky was dull and threatened to snow, which was not an impossibility in April.

The rooftops of the surrounding buildings were dingy and spotted with islands of dirty, icy, rock-hard snow piles that had once been swirls of fresh white powder snow, which over the course of the winter had collected in the shaded nooks and corners of the roof tops. Now, looking like packs of hardened sooty snow, they would probably last through May if they didn't get any direct sun.

Soot spewed endlessly out of the dozens of factory chimneys that towered above the heavy manufacturing plants that crowded Milwaukee's industrial valley, a valley carved out by the Milwaukee River sometime after the Ice Age. The soot landed on every surface in the city, not just the tops of buildings. The Milwaukee River meandered through the landscape of hundreds of docks and in and out of boat slips, like a river of mercury, adding yet another tone of gray to the view out the window. Shoreline ice on Lake Michigan hadn't begun to break up. It, too, was looking a dull gray, barely in contrast to the water and worn smooth, its jagged edges long gone from too many months of winter. It ran down the coast like an irregular gray ribbon as far as the eye could see, separating the gray, cold waters of the lake from the gray, cold real estate that hugged its boundary.

Dr. Dunker's whole mood was gray, like everything as far as he could see, as he contemplated his life in between the day's meetings with one patient after another. He didn't have much time to contemplate his situation. There were people in both patient rooms and two more impatiently waiting to see him in the reception area, and more expected. His receptionist, Delia, was busy orchestrating the flow of people in need of medical attention and all the forms that come with these visits. And LuAnne Tompkins, his nurse for the past ten years, had her hands full making sure that every patient had the proper care coming in and follow-up instructions going out, while assisting each patient's treatment every step of the way. Everyone was busy, too busy.

Dr. Dunker was too busy three days a week in his office and two days a week in St. Joseph's hospital, a workload that was burdened with some late night and weekend emergencies, but he rationalized that busy was good. Busy kept his mind off his personal life. Busy kept his mind off the tragedy of losing his wife, who had died two months ago. Busy kept his mind off the challenges of being a father to two small children who were now motherless. Thankfully, he had a nanny to take care of them, but the responsibilities of it all were quite overwhelming.

He loved his two children, Peggy and Steve, who were nine and seven years old. He knew they would need a mother sooner or later, and he would need a wife sooner or later, hopefully sooner. Was it too soon to think about that possibility, the possibility of another wife and mother in his home? Probably, he thought. He knew he still had a lot of grieving ahead of him, but the pragmatic side of him was equally sure that he couldn't go it alone for too long.

As a result of a couple of no-shows, the patient load finally eased up a bit in the final hour of an afternoon that was supposed to conclude at four o'clock, as it did every day. It was looking like the threesome had survived another frenetic day, although more than two hours of paperwork would keep Delia at her desk until at least six.

At three-thirty, a tall, rather striking woman walked into the office. Delia didn't recognize her, so she guessed she was the person who matched the new patient file on her desk. The very slight limp that this woman had didn't look to Delia like anything other than sore feet. The woman approached the desk's open reception window and said she had been referred to Dr. Dunker by a colleague of his in Fond du Lac, an ophthalmologist named Dr. Keitel. She told Delia that her name was Connie Koehler. Delia handed her a form and asked her to make herself comfortable in one of the chairs in the reception area while she was filling it out. Then, she assured her that Dr. Dunker would see her shortly. Having glanced at the file in advance, Delia's curiosity made her take a quick but careful look at Connie's left eye, the one the file had indicated was a prosthetic, and couldn't help thinking it looked pretty good. Keitel had done some good work, she thought to herself, before getting back to some pressing paperwork.

Twenty minutes later, Nurse Tompkins opened a door adjacent to Delia's reception office and invited Connie into a patient suite to prep her for Dr. Dunker's appearance. There wasn't any specific treatment required before the doctor showed up, but Nurse Tompkins wanted to get a quick preliminary understanding of any needs that might have to be met in that first visit and make sure that Connie wasn't in any discomfort. The sudden decline in workload gave Nurse Tompkins a chance to chat a bit with Connie, which was her practice with every new patient.

The two women took to each other right away and quickly discovered that they both came from the same part of the state—Connie from Chilton, of course, and LuAnne from Sheboygan. Their hometowns were only thirty-eight miles apart, which made the two small town girls think of each other as neighbors.

Connie told LuAnne that she had been working at Gimbels but was looking for an office position of sorts, something like filing—something that didn't require her to stand up all day long because of her bad leg. LuAnne was quick to see the possible match and told Connie that Dr. Dunker badly needed administrative help. She said she'd look into it and talk to the doctor. She promised she would call Connie sometime in the next couple of days to follow up. Just then, Dr. Dunker walked into the patient room and met Connie Koehler for the first time.

There are a lot of people out there who have been married for whatever length of time and claim that they experienced love at first sight or that they instantly felt they would marry the person they had just met. It must be purely chemistry because the attraction is often felt within the first minute or two of meeting, and maybe less time than that! Of course, an attraction doesn't mean anything will come of it; it just sends a shared signal that there is something in the meeting that should be explored. It has happened to me, and if it has happened to you, you surely know what I'm talking about. But I digress.

CHAPTER THIRTY-NINE

When Connie saw him for the first time, George Dunker was older than she had expected. He might have been forty—at least ten years older than her—although she didn't know why she had expected him to be younger. She knew from Dr. Keitel that he and Dr. Dunker were friends from their days at Marquette Medical School twenty years earlier. Dr. Keitel was forty, so it made sense. Dr. Dunker was also shorter than she had expected—maybe five-six, which was two inches shorter than her. She remembered that Dr. Keitel was tall, over six feet, like Carl. She liked tall men, but Dr. Dunker had a quality that she was drawn to right away—an air about him—and then it struck her that it was an air of competence. He seemed worldly, collected, focused, and maybe even—and this surprised her—a little sad. She liked him right away.

"You're Connie Koehler?" He pronounced Koehler like molar, with a long o.

She corrected him, "It's pronounced Koehler," Connie said it correctly, adding, "like tailor. It's German."

"I know. I'm German. I just wasn't sure." He smiled and totally surprised her when he half sang, "I say toe-may-toe; you say toe-mah-toe. Let's call the whole thing off." She recognized the lyrics from a Gershwin tune in the late thirties. She was suddenly surprised, as she thought she recognized a little flirting in his voice, just a teeny, teeny hint of it. His sad look fled, and suddenly his eyes were smiling. He opened her file and paged through some of the papers. Without looking up, he said, "I see from your file you've had quite a bit of trauma to your left eye. I understand it happened in a car accident." He paused and looked up at her, "I'm so sorry." And then he lingered on her face, a face that had some faint scars, barely discernible. And then, tilting his chin upward, specifically looked at her glass eye and added, "I already talked with Dr. Keitel about your injury. He spoke highly of you and said you'd done an amazing job of healing from your injuries."

"Oh, he has been so wonderful." Connie interjected and relaxed a bit. "He did so much for me."

"Yes," replied Dr. Dunker, searching her face, "I can see that. He's done some very good work." Dr. Dunker moved in closer, within inches of Connie's face, simultaneously pulling from the pocket of his lab coat a black, tubular metal instrument, which had a tiny spotlight that was coordinated with the magnification it provided. It was the only thing that separated their closeness. First, he looked into her good eye, gently holding up her lid with his free hand. Nurse Tompkins stood behind him with the file he had passed back to her, poised to take notes. He said somewhat absently, "uh-ha, yes, uh-ha," but nothing else about her good eye.

Connie noticed that he smelled like soap, and his breath was warm.

Dr. Dunker noticed her perfume but didn't know what it was. Whatever it was, he liked it. It momentarily distracted him from his doctor-patient focus, but only for a second. Then he moved in on the other eye, the glass one, and began looking at it and the area around it through that special instrument he was using. He gently moved his thumb around the orbital area of her eye, applying slight pressure to various places. "Any tenderness?" he asked softly, his breath washing over her while he stayed close in on her. He pulled back, straightened his posture, and asked, "Any pain ever?"

"No," Connie said, responding to both questions with a single answer, "other than it always feels like something that's in there, in my head, but not really me." He didn't respond to her comment directly. Connie continued, "but it doesn't really hurt, I mean, really hurt."

"It's a little dry in some areas," Dr. Dunker observed. "As Dr. Keitel noted, there was considerable trauma to your tear ducts," he said, indicating Connie's left eye. "Maybe causing a little discomfort from time to time, yes?" he turned his observation into a question.

"Uh-huh," Connie responded, "That's why I was anxious to see you. That and I need a doctor here in town, you know, for my eye." Connie was suddenly feeling self-conscious in her choice of words. She could feel her heart beating and was sure Dr. Dunker could hear it, given his closeness to her. She looked at LuAnne and, for no apparent reason, smiled at her before turning her attention back to the doctor.

"I'll prescribe another kind of ointment for you to use once a day and some more drops for your eye that you should apply four times daily or as needed. I'd like to see you again in two weeks, when I'll present some more ideas for making you more comfortable. There are some other things we can do." He turned to Nurse Tompkins and detailed the prescriptions and then abruptly walked out of the office without saying a word.

The appointment was over, and LuAnne led Connie back to the reception area for some follow-up paperwork with Delia. LuAnne stepped into Delia's office, which had sliding glass panels above her desk that were open, separating her workspace from the waiting room. Connie leaned forward, from the waiting room, slightly into the open window space overlooking Delia's desk. From over Delia's shoulder, LuAnne softly said, out of earshot of the waiting patients, "Connie, it was so nice meeting you. I'll call you in a couple of days about that job after I talk to the doctor."

"Thank you, LuAnne," Connie replied in a similarly soft tone, "Thank you so much for looking into that for me." And then she added with a smile, "I think I'd like to work here."

LuAnne picked up on something just then in Connie's tone and earlier in the office when Connie and Dr. Dunker had been together. She sensed some kind of electricity between the two of them because she couldn't help adding, "and I think Dr. Dunker would like you to work here too." She paused over what she thought might have sounded like an indiscretion and quickly added, "We really could use some extra help."

"Oh, one thing, LuAnne," Connie added while still leaning over the windowed countertop into Delia's space, "would you mind if I call you instead? I'm staying at the Catholic Women's Residence, the one on Farwell, and the rooms don't have phones. It might be difficult to get a message to me."

"Fine, call me on Friday at the end of day," LuAnne said, "I bet I'll have an answer for you then."

"Thanks, I will," she smiled at LuAnne and then Delia before turning and walking into the hallway and out of sight as the door closed behind her.

Delia leaned forward and slid the glass window closed for a moment of privacy and turned back to LuAnne, "What was that all about?"

"She's looking for a job," LuAnne replied, "something

administrative, where she doesn't have to stand on her feet all day."

"Lord knows we could use some help around here. I know that much," said Delia, "but like I said, what was that all about?"

"What was what all about?"

"LuAnne, you're holding back. You know what I mean. What was 'I think Dr. Dunker would like you to work here too?' all about?"

"Oh, that?"

"Yes, *that*!

"I don't know. There was just something about their meeting, you know, when the doctor walked in. I don't know— hard to explain. He might be interested in her."

"What! His wife died barely two months ago. Are you kidding?" Delia responded with a surprised, but conspiratorial, whisper.

"Who's to say how long is long enough? And I'm thinking that Connie Koehler might be interested in him! Hey, who am I to try to explain things? I'm just telling you what I saw. He'd be a lucky man," she added, "Despite her injuries, she's a good looking woman."

The hallway door opened, and Dr. Dunker stuck his head into Delia's office, causing an end to the speculation. "I'm ready!" he stated. "Both patient rooms are empty. Let's go!" he said, indicating a desire to get through the day and disappeared into the hallway as quickly as he had appeared. Only a few more patients and then the workday would end, but it would still be a gray day outside. Moments later, George Dunker stood at his office window once again, momentarily looking out over the expanse of gray in front of him. Nothing had changed—or had it?

Human nature is so fascinating. At times we exercise such gross insensitivity to other people's feelings that it's shocking. On the other hand, we can be incredibly sensitive. There are times when our senses pick up on the smallest, most miniscule vibration from another or between two people, one so minute that we can't be sure that there was any one event that enabled us to pick up on it. Even so, we still know that within us there is some mysterious innate sense to read people and to empathize, maybe even decipher their intentions. It is a sense that makes us believe that a certain event, however invisible, truly took place, one that allows us to draw a conclusion that we could bet on, as inexplicable as betting on the supernatural. But I digress.

CHAPTER FORTY

Connie called LuAnne two days after her appointment, as requested, and was suddenly ecstatic upon hearing the news that Dr. Dunker wanted her to work in the office as soon as possible. The pay was about the same as Gimbels, so Connie didn't hesitate to tell LuAnne that she'd give Gimbels two weeks notice and be ready to start the first week in May.

On Monday, May 2, 1949, Connie walked into Dr. Dunker's office at eight that morning, ready to work as the office's official Administrative Assistant. She greeted Delia and LuAnne, who were expecting her, as soon as she walked in. They told her that Dr. Dunker never showed up on Mondays and Tuesdays because those were his days for surgery or making the rounds at St. Joe's, which was on the near west side of town, so he wouldn't even be around.

Delia had allocated some space in the supply room for Connie, just enough for a small desk and some shelf space for files, which was created by shifting some bandage boxes and other medical supplies to another shelf. The space suited Connie just fine, and she was particularly pleased to discover that her chair, although made of hardwood, was actually quite comfortable. It was sure better than having to stand on her feet all day. The day got off to a good start for all three of them.

At three o'clock that afternoon, Dr. Dunker walked into the office, without warning.

"Hi," he said solemnly, in his busy man voice, startling LuAnne, as he entered through the front door. He just showed up, contrary to his habit of spending Mondays at the hospital. Delia and LuAnne looked at each other, sharing their surprise, both knowing that he hadn't been in the office on a Monday for years.

"Dr. Dunker!" replied a startled Delia. "Is anything wrong? You're supposed to be at St. Joe's."

"No," he said as he walked past her through the door into the hallway that connected his office with the patient rooms and the supply room. "Nothing's wrong, and St. Joe's doesn't need me this afternoon. I just wanted to get something out of my desk that I left behind last Friday." He went into his office and made a show of rummaging around in the contents of one of the drawers, when LuAnne stopped at his open door. "Dr. Dunker, are you sure everything's all right?"

"Oh, everything's fine," he said, as he looked up from behind his desk. "I just needed something from my desk for a meeting at the Yacht Club tonight." He liked to sail—she knew that—and the opening day at The Milwaukee Yacht Club was coming up. She thought his reply was plausible, but her feminine intuition told her there might be more going on.

"Oh, okay," she calmly replied. And before she could turn away, he asked her, "How's the new person working out?"

"Connie?"

"Yeah, Connie. How's she working out?"

With the exchange of those words, in a flash, LuAnne got it: he was there to see Connie. "Ha," she thought to herself, "he couldn't wait till Wednesday.... I wonder if Delia figured it out too." She nonchalantly replied, "It's only her first day, but I think things are going well. I think she's at her desk in the supply room at the moment. We set her up there this morning. Maybe you should say hi to her," and with the most neutral tone she could muster, she added, "I'm sure she'd like that."

"Yeah, sure," he said, and with the most neutral tone he could muster, he said, "I think I'll do that." He waited for LuAnne to leave and go do whatever she was doing before he closed his desk drawer and straightened his necktie and then headed for the supply room.

The door was open. Connie was moving some folders around and saw him as he approached. She knew that he was in the office. It was a relatively small place, and his male voice easily carried down the hallway. He walked a couple of feet into her office, stopping just inside the open door.

"Hello, Miss Koehler," he said somewhat solemnly and yet with a little playfulness in his eyes, making a point of using the correct pronunciation of her last name with a very slight intonation of exaggeration.

"Hi, Dr. Dunker!" she cheerily replied.

"I'm glad you decided to take the job," he said.

"Thank you for the chance. I won't disappoint you. Delia and LuAnne have already been a big help in getting me started. They said there's a lot to do."

"I'm sure there is."

"Oh, and please call me Connie."

"Okay, Connie, I will." He didn't return the favor of asking her to call him anything other than Dr. Dunker. He didn't feel it was appropriate, and suddenly he realized he'd have to be careful not to do anything that wasn't appropriate. He felt self-conscious again and a little charged upon seeing her, and in a moment of silence, realized she was waiting for him to say something. He cleared his throat, made a move to back out of the doorway, and then added, "Well, like I said, I'm glad you're here." With that, he turned and walked into the reception area and called out "Bye!" to Delia and LuAnne, who were standing side by side in Delia's office, making a show of going through a patient's file, but from the look on their faces, the thought occurred to him that they might be discussing something else.

He walked out of the office, making a mental note that he'd have to maintain his professional demeanor in the office at all times, even though that might not be so easy. When he stepped onto the elevator to leave the building, with no one else on board, he said softly to himself, "There's something about her that I like. Yep, there's something about Connie that I like a lot." He started to whistle. He often whistled absent-mindedly, especially when things were going his way.

In the following weeks, despite the separation of space created in the supply room, the addition of Connie to the staff made for closer quarters for everyone. She was continually moving back and forth between the supply room and Delia's office, where most of the records were stored. She took over the organization of the patient files and billing, both of which were responsibilities Delia was happy to shuck. Her movement in and out of the receptionist's office meant passing LuAnne and, on Wednesdays, Thursdays, and Fridays, passing Dr. Dunker in the hallway a dozen times a day.

With the new member on the staff, everyone's workload became more manageable and everyone became visibly happier. The biggest impact that Connie's presence had was on Dr. Dunker. He had become a different person with her in the office, and Delia and LuAnne had no doubt that the change in him was because of Connie. It might have been her upbeat attitude and constant cheer. She was clearly enjoying her responsibilities, and she was a quick study, which made her easy to work with. But the speculation continued—it certainly seemed that the doctor was infatuated with Connie.

Three weeks later, when Delia and LuAnne had stepped out for lunch and the office was without patients, the doctor and Connie were working at their desks. He rose from his desk, walked to his office window, and looked out over the downtown area and the industrial valley, as he had countless times. It was a perfect summer day, although summer hadn't officially started in his mind. Memorial Day weekend was the opening day at the Yacht Club, an exciting day for everyone at the club, and it was coming up this weekend. There wasn't a cloud in sight, and the temperature had freakishly risen into the upper seventies, a rarity for that time of year when the average temperatures were in the mid-sixties.

He spun on his heel, walked out of his office, turned down the hallway, and within a matter of seconds, was at the door to the supply room looking at Connie seated at her desk. He knew what he wanted to do and didn't want to waste time doing it, fearful that Delia or LuAnne would walk in any minute and interrupt a delicate moment in what he thought was a bold move.

Connie looked up, surprised to suddenly see him standing in her doorway. "Hi, Dr. Dunker, what can I do for you?"

He was not a man to mince words. "Will you let me take you out to dinner on Friday?" He had thought about this invitation all week and decided that Friday was the right night, a better night for a first date that weekend. Saturday night was the big opening day dinner at the Yacht Club. If they had fun on Friday, he'd ask her to be his guest at the club on Saturday.

Saturday, he decided, was too big of an event for a first date. He much preferred to have some quiet one-on-one time with her so that they could get to know each other better. Friday might give him that. Of course, he was aware that she might already have plans for Saturday night, but it was a risk he was willing to take.

Connie had been through too much in life to waste time being coy. "Okay," she replied without hesitating. "What time do you want to pick me up?"

"How 'bout seven?" he suggested.

"Okay."

"Catholic Women's Residence on Farwell?" he asked. He had done his homework.

"Yes, that's where I'm staying." She paused. He glanced over his shoulder, wondering if he had heard someone enter the reception area. "The Residence has a curfew, you know?" she added, once she had his attention again.

"No. What do you mean?"

"All women living there are required to be home by ten every night. You can't be a minute late."

"Okay," he said, "I can live with that. How 'bout if I pick you up at six instead? Give us one more hour together, okay?"

"Yes," she smiled, "that works for me." She didn't tell him it was her first date in over two years. She was sure he didn't know much about her personal life, although he knew, of course, that she had injured her eye in a car accident, but nothing else about that. Maybe Dr. Keitel had told him some things. She didn't know anything about his personal life, really, although she knew that his wife had died in February and left him with two little kids. That his wife had died so recently was something that had crossed her mind, and maybe it would have

198

bothered someone else that the loss was relatively recent. But Connie knew how tenuous life was and how fast things could change, and she had learned to focus more on the present than dwell on the past or, for that matter, dream about the future. If he was asking her out, then she thought he must be okay with the fairly recent passing of his wife.

Dr. Dunker and Connie both heard the main door open and guessed that Delia and LuAnne had just entered the reception area from the hallway. They were sure of it when lighthearted laughter suddenly penetrated every room in the suite, confirming Delia and LuAnne's return to work, thus, forcing the truncation of the intimate conversation.

Dr. Dunker furtively said, "See you Friday at six," and returned to his office. He went to the window to look out at the city and marvel over the wonderment of life and how the weather could change so quickly, gray one day and then gloriously sunny the next. Connie already knew that life worked that way, and in the bigger picture, she knew it worked both ways.

Love has more facets than the Great Star of Africa, the largest cut diamond in the world. If someone else hasn't said that already, then consider it said right now. The first cut sometimes begins with no more than a shadow overlaid on a rough gem, but it is nonetheless the beginning no matter how subtle or obscure. Love puts atoms in motion in ways that take them beyond their usual movement and can cause behavior that is so contrary to previous patterns that there can be no other explanation for that behavior other than love, or the first cut of it anyway. But I digress.

CHAPTER FORTY-ONE

George climbed out of his Cadillac, walked around its frontend, and opened the door for Connie. He then put his arm around her and walked her to the front door of the Catholic Women's Residence at ten minutes to ten, beating her curfew with minutes to spare. Once at the threshold, they faced each other.

"Goodnight George. I had a wonderful time." She liked calling him George, although they had agreed that she would continue to address him as Dr. Dunker in the office. "Silly," she thought, "but sensible."

"Goodnight Connie. I had a wonderful time too." They were face to face, two feet apart. His left hand held her right hand, and his right hand held her left hand, in a pose that wedding couples take at the alter during their vows. Neither spoke; they just looked at each other as if they could see beyond the aqueous humor, the limpid fluid within the eyeball between the cornea and the lens, and maybe beyond, into the initial depths of each other's essence, to a place where they both wanted to take a deeper dive into each other.

For a moment, for both of them, time stopped, and all intrusions from the outside world ceased. For that matter, everything about the outside world had ceased. The only world that existed that very moment was the space they shared and the oneness they felt in that space. Poets would say their hearts beat as one, and physiologically, that actually might have been true at that moment.

Earlier that evening, over dinner at Mader's restaurant, which was George's favorite place, both of them had taken a big chance in their first encounter in telling each other their personal stories. That kind of exposure on a first date often doesn't work; it carries too much information to process, too many feelings to make sense of, too many vulnerabilities to accept, and too much meaning that is absent of context. But for them, it worked perfectly. They felt an instant and deep attraction, something much more meaningful than most people experience on a first date, or even a twentieth one. Even if they couldn't understand it, a bonding experience had occurred that evening, and they both had had enough experience in life to have no doubt that it was love that drew them together, and it was real.

What they didn't understand at the time, but what they would come to understand later, is that they were two people who were drawn to each other through a profound shared sense of the deeply felt loss of a beloved spouse. Their broken hearts fit each other perfectly.

George looked at his watch, breaking the intensity they had been sharing for several minutes at the top of the steps. "It's one minute before ten. You'd better ring." He reluctantly let go of her right hand. She reached out and rang the doorbell, which was already close to her fingertips. Within seconds, she was buzzed into the building's foyer. In the blink of an eye, Connie kissed George on the cheek and slipped as softly as a summer breeze through the open door, spun around for a second before it closed, looked at George, who hadn't moved, and reminded him, "See you at six tomorrow night!" Then she walked down the hallway, turned left, and was out of his sight, but fully in his heart, as he was in hers.

That was the beginning of a whirlwind romance. Six months later, on Christmas Day, 1949, George proposed marriage to Connie, and Connie said yes. They were married June 10, 1950 at St. Mary's Catholic Church in Chilton. By the way, Virginia Stranski, the mother of an eight month-old baby girl, was Connie's maid of honor, for the second time.

Life is so interesting. There are so many possibilities. It is safe to say that the possibilities are not only countless, but many are beyond our imagination. We might have one life to live, but we can actually live many lives in a single lifetime. Some are lucky enough to share much of one lifetime with one other individual in connubial bliss. But for many others, for various reasons, that doesn't happen. However, sometimes we get another shot at living life blissfully in love. And sometimes that happens just when we thought it was most unlikely. Love may be elusive, but it's out there. I'm pretty sure of that, sometimes. But I digress.

CHAPTER FORTY-TWO

George and Connie honeymooned for a week at the regal Grand Hotel on Mackinac Island, a small rustic island between Michigan and Michigan's upper peninsula, where cars are forbidden. It was a timelessly classic hotel, open only in the summers. For George and Connie, it meant the end of forbidden fruit.

On June 18, 1950, when they returned to Milwaukee, they moved into their new house in Fox Point, a wealthy suburb that ran up the shoreline of Lake Michigan about eight miles north of downtown Milwaukee. While they had been gone, George's children, Peggy and Steve, had stayed with his sister, who also lived in Milwaukee. Now, the family of four would live under one roof, looking as much like any traditional American family of four could look, although this was one that lived better than most. It would be an arduous but fun week of turning a house into a home. Boxes were piled in every room and completely took over the garage. All would eventually be opened and their precious contents allocated to the right rooms, closets, shelves, nooks, and crannies.

Connie had been dreaming about this for months and, actually, every day since her engagement to George, and now—on this very day—it was real. She was now married to a wonderful man and she had two children to care for. Her dream had come true. It was the dream of a lifetime. It was only two years ago that she had thought the dream was over, that it could never happen, that she would never be loved by another man, and now she was a wife—and a mother! Even if she could never have children of her own, she had George's two children to take of—they needed a mother, and she would be a mother to them.

Being a wife and mother were the only two things she had ever truly wanted in life. Now she was both, and as she stood in the bedroom of their new house, surrounded by furniture, large moving boxes, and stacks and stacks of smaller cartons, tears of joy ran down her cheeks. She looked around the room... all these boxes and not a single box of Kleenex! She went to her sleeves, took a couple of deep breaths, got control of her tears, and with a smile on her face for the silliness of all those tears, began unpacking again.

George was opening the boxes for the kids in their bedrooms, while Connie was working in the master bedroom. She cut off the packing tape of one very large box and tugged open the flaps. It had been consigned to the master bedroom and had "master closet" written on it. She was expecting it to be full of George's clothes—suits, she imagined—as it was the kind of a box that resembled a closet in a box. It did have a lot of suits in it, all hanging on a dull metal bar that ran through the top of the box. She reached over the flaps of the tall box and pulled a couple of suits out, hung them up in the closet, and returned to the box to pull out a couple more.

As she made a second grab at hangers, she saw something in the bottom of the box that completely surprised her and caught her immediate attention. It was a bundle of fur, possibly a fur coat; she couldn't tell without removing a few more suits and pulling the mystery item out of the bottom of the box.

Anxious to understand what the furry item was, she quickly pulled George's suits off the metal bar, two at a time in each hand, and set them on the floor. She was staring down at what looked like a blanket of mink, rolled up in the bottom of the box. She pushed the box over on its side, lifted the bottom upward, and watched a big mink coat slide onto the floor. Speechless, she pushed the box aside and stood over the coat for a few seconds staring down at this big surprise that was clumped at her feet. Just then, George walked into the room.

"I see you found Connie's mink coat." Connie knew he was referring to his first wife, who coincidentally had been named Connie. George leaned over the coat, groped it for the inside of the back collar, and lifted it, feigning a grunt over its bulk. It was a lot of fur, and Connie quickly went into an expression of total surprise, although shock might more accurately describe the feeling behind her surprise.

"Oh my God, George!" Connie exclaimed as she, unbeknownst to George, realized that she had seen that coat before.

"Yeah," George quickly reacted to Connie's surprise. "It's a big ball of fur! I hope you don't mind, but I wanted to save it—for you. I want you to have it. Is that okay?"

Connie was speechless as she recalled the one and only time she had seen that coat. She was sure it was the same one because she had never seen a coat with such large cuffs before. It never occurred to her, of course, that the Connie she had met that afternoon in Gimbels two winters ago was George's Connie—his first wife! Connie easily recalled that one meeting. That poor woman, Connie remembered, had said she had cancer and was taking treatments for it. "Oh my God!" Connie exclaimed to George again, as the whole scene at

Gimbels came back to her as if it had been yesterday. The last thing the woman had said to her was, "I hope someday I can return the favor."

"It's beautiful, isn't it?" said George, convinced that Connie was simply being overwhelmed by the coat's exquisite beauty. Holding the coat up and open for her to slip into, he added, "Here, try it on."

Connie backed slowly into the coat. Her mind raced, as she wondered if she should tell George the story or not. She decided not to. It didn't seem to be the right time to tell him— maybe some other time.

George hefted it onto her shoulders. "Try that," he said, triumphantly, clearly happy to have this beautiful coat worn by his new, beautiful wife.

She stepped away from him and modeled it with a twirl one way and then a twirl the other way, smiling at George for the wonderful gift and now smiling with the bittersweet memory of its original owner, whose gift to her was even greater than the most beautiful mink coat Connie had ever seen.

Sometimes I think that if I had known that the world was so small when I was younger, I might have behaved differently, not that I have behaved poorly, mind you, but few people would disagree that living in a small community, like Chilton, makes people think twice before engaging in questionable, insensitive, or unkind behavior. There is less scrutiny in a big city, like New York, where it is easier to lead a life of anonymity. Wherever we live, the idea of six degrees of separation is a good thing to keep in mind. It postulates that we are all connected to each other by as little as six other people; thus, the world is actually quite small—certainly not as small as Chilton, but small. Good behavior makes sense, and being nice to everyone makes particularly good sense. Most importantly, we feel better about ourselves when we are nice to everyone. But I digress.

CHAPTER FORTY-THREE

It was a scorcher, as they say in Wisconsin, in the back half of July, right when you would expect one. It was a Saturday, and the clock had just struck twelve. The temperature was already at eighty-one degrees, and the morning passed without a breeze of any kind. The temperature would surely go up a few more degrees in the next couple of hours.

George and Connie were on the flagstone patio in the backyard, relaxing in the heat under the cool shade of a couple of big elm trees. They looked out on a lush backyard that was defined by rock walls on the sides and a white picket fence on the back lot line, which separated them from another house tucked under the shade of more giant elm trees. Peggy and Steve were playing at the neighbor's house a block away on Lake Drive. In this heat, they were either in the swimming pool or carousing on the beach and splashing around in Lake Michigan's chilly waters. Lucky them!

George was working on his umpteenth Camel cigarette and his second cold beer, a long neck bottle of Schlitz, "the beer that made Milwaukee famous." He had worked up a shirt-soaking sweat from a full morning of planting and replanting in the flower beds that ran the length of the rock walls, mostly Fiddlehead ferns he had collected from the woodsy property around his summer home on Big Cedar Lake the weekend before.

Connie had an iced tea in front of her, but she wasn't drinking it. She didn't even feel like sipping it. She didn't feel like conversation or much of anything for that matter. She sighed, but not the sigh of contentment; it was closer to a sigh of discomfort, and George picked up on it.

"You okay, honey?" he inquired.

"Yeah, just feeling… I don't know, a little queasy maybe," she responded in slow motion, unable to shuck off the oppressive heat.

"Maybe the heat's getting to you," George offered. "Try drinking your iced tea. You might feel better—it's hot. When it's this hot, the body needs lots of fluids." He scanned the yard and liked what he saw. Many of the flowers were in full bloom. The tiger lilies were blooming by the dozens in the beds in the corners at the far end of the backyard. He had transported them from the house on Cedar Lake two months ago. He was happy to see that they were doing well. They were nice reminders of how much he loved Big Cedar Lake. His thoughts wandered in the stillness of the day, and within moments, he was at the lake with his memories.

The lake house had been built thirty-five years ago by his father, on the east side of a pristine lake about forty miles northwest of Milwaukee. That was Big Cedar Lake, which overshadowed the one next to it, Little Cedar Lake. It was a humble lake home—more cottage than house—consistent with other dwellings on the shoreline, with its best feature being a very large screened porch, which is where life in the cottage happened most. The property was adjacent to a working farm, which guaranteed the cottage dwellers fresh eggs every morning, in this sacred place of solitude on the shoreline of a tree-lined lake with water clarity that was so good you could easily see the bottom at twenty-five feet.

The fishing was easy and the sailing could be vigorous, although the lake wasn't really very big, despite the name. The Cedar Lake Yacht Club was directly across the lake, about a half mile to the other side. Dock-sitting was pleasant, and it was easy to sit for hours and watch the lightning class sailboats sail in and out of the Yacht Club, like bees at a hive, and zig-zag around the lake. Sightings of ski boats trailing water skiers were climbing with the passage of summers. Their buzz, like summer's cicadas, was intrusive. Between weekly thunder-storms, the gentle lapping of water on the rocks that trimmed the fern-crested shoreline was particularly pleasant and had lulled more people into a nap on the dock chairs than anyone could count.

George happily recalled the annual summer parties at the lake house, where each year his father, Oscar Dunker, and his father's band, Dunker's Band, would set up on the front lawn for a day of music with John Phillip Sousa and countless other American favorites. The band of forty men would arrange themselves in concentric semi-circles, and Oscar would conduct, his baton in constant motion, standing tall while dressed in his white waistcoat with a design on it of a black staff of notes. He always wore a silk top hat, and everyone thought that was a grand touch.

At these events, boats lined the shoreline and cars filled the fields, emptied from discharging the hundreds of people who attended. This was big entertainment for a country lake house in rural Wisconsin and something that was always remembered by those who attended, whether they had been there thirty times or only once. Since George couldn't recall ever having missed that special annual event, for him, that would be forty-one times. What a great day for kids. "Yeah," he thought to himself, "Cedar Lake was a great place for kids."

With a break in his thoughts, George stared blankly for a minute at the peonies he had just planted, surprised that their blooms were already so full. He had put them in the ground in the spring when the house was still under construction and wasn't sure they'd even bloom this summer. They looked terrific. He liked peonies a lot; they reminded him of his youth. His mom had had a long garden of them on the west side of their house—pink and white ones. She loved them too and always marveled over the size of their magnificent blossoms, blossoms so big that the stems often fell over with their weight. His were white; he didn't think he could do pink.

Connie thought about the heat for a minute and about how she felt and took her time responding to George's suggestion to drink her iced tea.

"I'm not really thirsty," she finally concluded, "… just a little queasy. I felt a little like this yesterday… and it wasn't nearly this hot then."

George laughed.

Connie asked, "What's so funny?"

"Nothing," he chuckled, to himself and then sat up straight, "… Jesus Almighty!" he cried out.

"Jesus Almighty what, George?"

He turned to look at her and waited till she looked at him before saying, "Maybe you're pregnant!"

"No," she said without hesitation. "You know that's not possible. I told you I couldn't get pregnant because of the accident." She always referred to that traumatic experience as "the accident."

George didn't let up. "Maybe you've got morning

sickness."

"But it's not the morning."

"Morning has nothing to do with it. Women can have morning sickness any time of the day, not just the morning."

"Really?" she asked. "That's true?"

"Yes, you bet that's true," he paused. "I don't know. Maybe it's the heat, or maybe not," he added, relaxing back into his chair before adding, "You know doctors can be wrong."

"Since when, DOCTOR George Dunker, has that ever been the case?"

"Well, I'm not one of them, of course," he responded with a smile, "but, hey, doctors can be wrong, like I said."

Connie said nothing and just sat there in silence, looking out over the yard. "Good God," Connie thought to herself, "Maybe he's right. Maybe I'm pregnant." That possibility had never occurred to her because it seemed to be an impossibility for her because of what the doctors had told her after she'd come out of the coma. It was something she had never thought about because it made her too sad to think that she couldn't have a baby. "Maybe it was morning sickness," she pondered.

"George," Connie exclaimed, "maybe I *am* pregnant!" She felt her heart leap with joy over the possibility, a joy that came out of nowhere, a joy she thought could never be hers. What she'd thought was impossible just became a possibility. But then doubt quickly moved in. She was amazed at how high her hopes had suddenly soared and then realized she had overreacted to what was possibly not at all the case. She realized, too, that she had just set herself up for one big whopping disappointment. Maybe it was the heat. And for a brief moment, she prayed it was the heat that was making her feel queasy. She could deal with that explanation. She wasn't sure she could deal with all of the emotions that would come with a pregnancy after accepting that it would never happen to her.

George interrupted her thoughts. "Come down to St. Joe's Monday morning, meet me, and we'll find out together."

"Yeah," she said, "let's do that." Connie stood up. "I'm going in the house to lie down for a while. Maybe I'll feel better a little later." She left her glass of iced tea on the table and went into the house, not having the energy or inclination to carry the glass in with her.

George didn't move except for reaching for his beer and taking another sip. The possibility of having another child hit him too. And he loved it. Right away, he loved the idea and hoped, indeed, that Connie was pregnant, although there was room for doubt of course. After all, he had just tossed the possibility into the ring as a lark of wishful thinking, no more than that. He knew that Connie had been told by doctors that having a baby was not at all likely and possibly even dangerous, but danger was a thought he dismissed. "How could that be?" he asked and made a mental note to talk to an OB about that.

He thought it through: "If she is pregnant, well, that's really something! I hope it's a boy. I'd like another boy." Then he said aloud to himself, "Yeah, I hope it's a boy" and made another mental note not to express a preference to Connie… that is, if she is pregnant. "Wow!" he said to himself, with a big sigh of contentment, "life is full of surprises." And then he went back to staring at the huge, white peony blossoms and losing himself in his childhood memories.

Two days later at St. Joe's hospital, Connie learned that she was indeed pregnant. George had been right. They guessed that conception had occurred five weeks ago, which placed the couple at The Grand Hotel for their honeymoon. At St. Joe's, they met with Dr. Servis to discuss concerns that Connie's accident might create complications. Records were reviewed, and Dr. Servis did what he could in examining Connie and exploring the possible ramifications that a pregnancy presented to her health.

The fact was that Connie was pregnant, and there was no choice other than to have the baby. And if it meant a risk to Connie's health, well, it was understood as a risk, but the birth would happen—that was what everyone expected. The unavoidable course of action made George a little nervous; he certainly didn't want to lose Connie. Connie reassured him over and over that having the baby was the right thing to do. She wanted a baby more than anything else and brushed aside any concerns that it was risky. Dr. Servis didn't see any obvious red flags, and so they would move forward and hope for the best.

The months passed and, with them, the seasons passed too. Life was good, and George and Connie were happy and so were the two kids. The due date was only three weeks away, and the excitement that had been building slowly over the previous eight months was now increasing exponentially. Would it be a boy or a girl? No one knew nor could know; there was just no way of telling. And, of course, would mom make it through the delivery all right? That was George and Connie's biggest concern, although no one was talking about that.

Of course they discussed names. George and Connie decided to name the baby John if it was a boy, after Connie's father, John Ortlieb, and Virginia, if it was a girl, after Connie's sister. If it was a girl, they would call her Ginny, for short.

We know from George's earlier soliloquy that he was privately hoping for a boy. It's funny how that works because Connie was privately hoping for a girl. Neither knew what the other was hoping for, and neither thought it a good idea to reveal their preference, so they concurrently said to each other that it didn't matter: each simply wanted a healthy baby delivered into the world, along with a mom that made it through the birth with no complications.

Couples actually function that way quite a bit through a first pregnancy—neither expresses a preference, and both operate with a desire for harmony and in avoidance of unnecessary conflict. Couples operate this way quite possibly through every pregnancy, and possibly, the same strategy applies to a lot of controversial issues that come up between two people in the course of a relationship, thus enabling them to move forward in life. In this way, I guess you can see the sensibility in all of this and, when the outcome is determined, simply say it was a matter of two hearts beating as one. It happens all the time. But I digress.

CHAPTER FORTY-FOUR

Connie gave birth shortly after midnight on March 15, 1951, and it appeared that she had survived, surprisingly, with no complications. She was sedated going in, owing to the potential for complications and pain, but Dr. Servis was confident that she would come out of it in the morning with no problems and that she would be happy with the outcome. George was with her through the birth and then spent the night in the hospital, something he'd done many times while meeting his obligations as a surgeon at St. Joe's. He wanted to be with her when she woke up from the sedatives. Earlier that night, Peggy and Steve had been taken in by a neighbor moments before George and Connie had left for the hospital. They would be anxiously awaiting the news, wanting to know if they had a baby brother or a baby sister. Peggy hoped for a sister and Steve hoped for a brother.

Early in the morning, two hours or so after the sun rose, Dr. Servis met the couple at Connie's bedside, with George at her side, holding her hand across the bed from him. The sedation had worn off, and Connie was alert, although a bit tired. The three of them discussed all the good news, including names. Then Dr. Servis left the two of them to be alone with each other to allow them the opportunity to let it all sink in.

George, still at her side, clasped Connie's hand closest to him in both of his, beaming with pride and comforting her.

"Again," he said, "I want you to know that more than anything I was worried about you. More than anything I wanted you to come through all this. And you did! Thank God for that! And thank God for everything. It's all a miracle!"

Connie looked into George's eyes the whole time. She, too, thought it was a miracle and an outcome she had never fully expected. "Yes, it's a miracle," she whispered in agreement, understandably fatigued.

George said, "So, you're okay with not naming him John and calling him Thomas instead?"

"Oh yes, darling," Connie purred. "Thomas was always a name I liked, but now it just seems right. It's so perfect."

"It is perfect, since it means 'twin,'" George said.

"Just think, George, we have twins—Tommy and Ginny."

George said, "I love it… Tommy and Ginny... the twins… Tommy and Ginny," he repeated the names, looking deeply into Connie's eyes as the names rolled off his lips. He loved her so much, and she loved him back. Those big empty spaces they had in their hearts from the loss of a spouse were no longer so big.

Connie nodded and, smiling, said one more time, "How perfect! Can I see them now?"

"They're on their way," George answered, "One of the nurses will be walking in with them any minute now."

Connie smiled in anticipation, feeling happier than she had ever dreamed possible.

In 1951, there wasn't any technology that could determine what the gender of a baby was during the mother's pregnancy. So the birth of twins was often a total surprise. This happens when two hearts beat as one. Yes, how perfect! But, this time, I am not digressing. That's my story, or maybe I should say, that's my mother's story.

EPILOGUE

Connie was married to George Dunker, M.D. until his death in 1977. He died of cancer of the throat. They lived together and raised four children in the same house on Berkeley Boulevard in Fox Point, a suburb on the north side of Milwaukee, for the twenty-seven years of their marriage. One year after his death, Connie eloped to London with Warren Callear, after which they returned to a life in Milwaukee. As husband and wife, Warren and Connie lived happily together. Seven years after their marriage, Warren was killed in a car accident. Connie died in Milwaukee in 1997 of cancer. Her twins were at her side when she died. She was buried in Chilton, Wisconsin, as she had requested, next to her mother Ruby Steenport.

ABOUT THE AUTHOR

Thomas Dunker was born in Milwaukee, Wisconsin and has lived in New York, Atlanta, Dallas, San Francisco, Napa, Scottsdale, and now lives in Sedona, Arizona. Besides being a writer, he is also an actor, an artist, and a marketing research consultant specializing in focus group moderation for Thomas Dunker & Associates, Inc. He paints under the name Tomaso DiTomaso: www.TomasoPaintings.com.

OTHER BOOKS BY THOMAS DUNKER

The following books by Thomas Dunker are available on Amazon.com:

Confessions of a Dating Fool

Confessions of a Dating Fool is twelve short stories of dates written by a man confessing to his own must-be-shared dating experiences. In these amazing stories, based on actual experiences, the author bares his soul, shares his thoughts, and takes the reader with him on every meaningful step of each date in settings all around the world. Several readers have described it as *Sex and the City* from a man's point of view. Many have also called it a light, entertaining read that's totally captivating, making it a real page turner.

A common denominator of many of these stories is a surprising outcome. The element of surprise in the dating world is something everyone who has ever dated can relate to. The immense diversity in the human genome assures us that every date is an adventure into the limitless world of human emotions. These stories are funny, moving, adventurous, and even tragic. Some include sex, of course, as this is a book of confessions. Some also include the promise of sex and even the avoidance of it, much akin to everyone's dating experiences. This book takes the reader on a rollercoaster ride right through the last paragraph.

Dating stories, especially good ones of bad dates, are irresistible and often told again and again. *Confessions of a Dating Fool* is a very light and quick read that has generated many a good laugh, a tear or two, and some terrific reader reviews on Amazon.com.

The Savvy Man's Guide to Finding True Love

The Savvy Man's Guide to Finding True Love is based on the author's interesting and refreshing point of view formed from years of experience in the dating world. It is a simple guidebook for men over thirty-nine years old who are interested in finding true love, or a life partner. It helps them realize that they may have been looking for love in all the wrong places by providing a better understanding of the importance of seeking like-minded women with similar life contexts. This light read postulates that the best woman for a man who is at least forty years old is a single mother who is at least 40 years old. There are many single men and women 40+ years old who are interested in true love. For men 40+, their search for true love is often misdirected toward younger women. For women 40+, there is a desire to have the men in their age group see the light and pleasure that they can provide, having life assets that younger, single, non-mothers simply don't have.

A NOTE FROM THE AUTHOR'S TWIN SISTER

To Tom from Ginny: I think you did a beautiful job capturing the intensity and poignancy of the tragedy that mom experienced. Your telling of her story has really touched me and also brought home the reality of mom's experience. When we were growing up, I often resented hearing about "the accident." This story has helped me understand what an enormous challenge this was to go through in her early life, and of course it affected her forever, even on her death bed, when she said, "I've suffered so." I hated hearing about her suffering, but it was true, and we have been so blessed in our lives to not ever have had a tragedy like this. I was resting today, and I intuitively received the message that mom feels she is being "honored" by you writing this, and it makes her very happy. How sweet!

ABOUT THE COVER ARTIST

Linnea Pergola is the artist who did the art on the cover of this book. She currently resides in Sedona, Arizona with her two golden retrievers, Beau and Blaze. She has been a professional artist her entire adult life and is very successful in a variety of media. She is also a world traveler and draws great inspiration from her travels. For a look at her work, please visit her website at: www.LinneaPergola-art.com.

AUTHOR'S NOTE

You might like to know that I will be happy to hear from you. It is best to simply email me. I can be quite good about returning emails. However, do not include attachments. I never open them. My email is ThomasJDunker@aol.com.

If you like my book, tell a friend. Better yet, buy a copy for a friend. People should know that authors love it when their books are purchased; it's so preferable to being asked for a copy. I will, of course, be happy to sign a copy for you. All you have to do is buy a copy, mail it to me with a check in the amount of $10 for shipping and handling and I'll see that you get the copy back with my signature and maybe a nice note along with it. My mailing address is P.O. Box 2189, Sedona, AZ 86339. Expect to wait 3-4 weeks for a signed copy to get back to you. Make your check payable to Thomas Dunker.